life
ceremony

Also by Sayaka Murata

Earthlings

Convenience Store Woman

life
ceremony

stories

sayaka
murata

Translated from the Japanese
by Ginny Tapley Takemori

Grove Press
New York

Originally published as *Seimeishiki*. Original Japanese edition published
by Kawade Shobo Shinsha, Ltd., Tokyo. English language translation
rights reserved to Grove Atlantic, Inc. under license granted
by Sayaka Murata arranged with Kawade Shobo Shinsha, Ltd.
through The English Agency (Japan) Ltd.

Published simultaneously in Canada
Printed in the United States of America

This book was set in 11-pt. Berling LT Std
by Alpha Design and Composition of Pittsfield, NH.
Designed by Norman E. Tuttle at Alpha Design & Composition

First Grove Atlantic hardcover edition: July 2022

Library of Congress Cataloging-in-Publication data is available for this title.

ISBN 978-0-8021-5958-8
eISBN 978-0-8021-5959-5

Grove Press
an imprint of Grove Atlantic
154 West 14th Street
New York, NY 10011

JAPANFOUNDATION 国際交流基金
Grove Atlantic gratefully acknowledges the support from
the Japan Foundation for this publication.

Distributed by Publishers Group West
groveatlantic.com

22 23 24 25   10 9 8 7 6 5 4 3 2 1

Contents

A First-Rate Material   1

A Magnificent Spread   21

A Summer Night's Kiss   45

Two's Family   49

The Time of the Large Star   59

Poochie   63

Life Ceremony   69

Body Magic   111

Lover on the Breeze   129

Puzzle   139

Eating the City   173

Hatchling   211

life
ceremony

A First-Rate Material

It was a holiday, and I was enjoying chatting with two girlfriends from university days over afternoon tea. Through the window, the gray office buildings of the business district sat beneath a cloudless sky. Reservations at this hotel lobby tearoom were hard to come by, and it was thronged with a female clientele. An elegant white-haired lady with a deep purple stole across her shoulders daintily carried a piece of tart to her mouth. At the table next to us, some girls with colorful painted nails were taking photos of their cakes. One of them spilled apricot jam on her white cardigan and hastily started wiping it off with a pink handkerchief.

Yumi opened the menu and ordered a second cup of tea, then noticed the sweater I was wearing.

"Hey, Nana, that sweater . . . is it human hair?"

"Oh, can you tell?" I beamed at her, nodding. "Yes, one hundred percent."

"Fantastic! It must have been expensive."

"Yeah, a bit . . . I took out a loan. But it'll last me for life," I answered rather bashfully, lightly running my fingertips over the garment. The jet-black hair was closely knitted into rows of braids, with an intricate weave at the cuffs and neck, and it glistened alluringly in the rays of light shining in through the lobby windows. Even though it was mine, it was so beautiful, and I gazed at it, enraptured.

Aya was eyeing it enviously too. "A hundred percent human hair is just the thing for winter! Warm, durable, and luxurious. My sweater contains some too, but it's so expensive I could only afford it mixed with wool. But human hair really does feel completely different, doesn't it?"

"Thanks. It's too special to wear every day, and normally I keep it safely stored away, but today I really wanted to dress up—it's the first time we've seen each other for ages, and coming to a hotel, too."

"Really? But now that you've bought it, it's such a waste not to wear it more," Yumi said.

Aya agreed. "Expensive clothes are not meant to simply decorate your closet, you know. You have to put them to good use! Nana, you're engaged to be married now, aren't you? Human hair is just the thing to wear for formal occasions, like meeting your future in-laws."

I toyed with my teacup. "Well, yes, but . . ." I said in a small voice. "You see, my fiancé doesn't really like clothes made from human hair."

"Whaaat?" Aya's eyes widened in bewilderment. "Why on earth not? I can't understand that!"

"I can't either, but it's not just human hair—he doesn't like any fashion accessories or furnishings made from human materials," I said, forcing a smile.

"You're kidding!" Shocked, Yumi put the macaroon she'd been about to put in her mouth back on her plate and looked at me dubiously. "So, what about bone rings? Tooth earrings?"

"He can't stand them. We're talking about making our wedding rings platinum, too."

Aya and Yumi looked at each other.

"Really? But wedding rings made from front teeth are the best!"

"Nana, your fiancé's a banker, isn't he? He must be well-off, so isn't he just being stingy?"

"No, I don't think it's that . . ." I answered vaguely, and smiled. I couldn't explain it very well myself.

Aya nodded triumphantly. "Yes, there are people like that who are loaded but just don't understand fashion . . . but Naoki's always so well-dressed, I'd never have expected it of him. When it comes to your wedding rings, though, I'd discuss that with him a bit more. After all, they're what you'll be using to pledge your eternal love for each other." She raised her teacup to her mouth. On her left hand was a ring made from pure white bone, her wedding ring, made from a fibula for her marriage last year, and it looked really good on her slender finger. I still clearly remembered how envious I'd felt when she'd happily shown it off to me, even while explaining that it was considerably cheaper than tooth.

I surreptitiously stroked my ring finger. The truth was that I did want a ring made from either tooth or bone. I'd talked about this any number of times with Naoki, and I knew better than anyone how futile it was.

"Look, go once more to the shop together. If he can just see what it looks like on his finger, he'll change his mind, you know."

I gave a little nod, looked down to avoid their eyes, and reached for the now-cold scone on my plate.

I'd just said goodbye to Aya and Yumi when I felt my cell phone vibrate. I took it from my bag and saw that an email had arrived from Naoki, who'd had to go in to work even though it was a holiday.

Got away earlier than I thought. How about coming over?

Okay, I replied, and got on a subway headed for his place.

He lived in a neighborhood close to where he worked, with office blocks alongside conveniently located residential condos. Once we were married, we planned to move to a new house in the suburbs, where there was a more natural environment better suited to kids. I was looking forward to living there, but felt a little sad at the thought that I wouldn't be returning to this neighborhood, where I'd spent so much time over the five years we'd been dating.

I rang the bell, and Naoki's amiable voice came through the interphone telling me to come in, so I opened the door with my key.

He must have only just arrived home since he was still in his shirt and tie, with a cardigan over his shoulders, and was turning on the underfloor heating.

"I bought dinner on the way," I said. "It's cold outside, so I thought hotpot would be good."

"Sounds great, thanks. How were the girls?"

"They're both fine. They gave us an engagement present."

I passed him the bag containing the pair of wineglasses from Aya and Yumi, put down my purse and the bag of groceries, and took off my duffle coat. His smile instantly vanished, replaced by a scowl.

Seeing the undisguised revulsion on his face, I remembered that I was still wearing the sweater.

"Didn't I tell you not to wear human hair?" he said in a low voice, avoiding my eyes, his face turned away from me so forcefully I thought his neck might snap as he plonked himself onto the couch.

"Um, well, I hadn't seen my friends for ages, and I wanted to impress them. I haven't worn it at all lately, and I thought it wouldn't do any harm to wear it just this once."

"You should throw it away. You promised me you wouldn't wear it. Have you gone back on your word?"

"But I haven't even paid off the loan yet. I promised I wouldn't wear it in front of you, but I never said I wouldn't ever wear it again. Why am I being told off for wearing something I bought with my own money?"

I choked up in spite of myself, and Naoki avoided looking at me as he drummed his fingers irritably on the floor.

"It gives me the creeps."

"But why? It's no different from your hair, or mine. It's more natural for us than hair from any other animal—it's a material really close to us."

"Yeah, that's exactly why it creeps me out," he spat, picking up a packet of cigarettes and a small ashtray from the side table.

Naoki hardly ever smoked, and he only ever reached for his cigarettes when he was really stressed and irritable and needed to calm himself down. I always did my best to comfort him whenever he lit up after work, complaining about being tired, but this time it was my fault he was feeling like this—just because of what I was wearing, I thought miserably.

"You're going to Miho's shop to look at new furniture tomorrow, aren't you?" he said, puffing out smoke. "I can't go along, so I'll leave it up to you, but let's get one thing straight—if you choose even just one item made from human products, I won't marry you. Teeth, bones, and skin are all out. Otherwise I'll break off the engagement."

"Talk about a unilateral decision. What could be more normal than making people into clothes or furniture after they die? How come you've got such an aversion to it?"

"It's sacrilegious! I can't believe you're so unfazed by using items hacked from dead bodies."

"Is using other animals any better? This is a precious and noble aspect of the workings of our advanced life-form—not wasting the bodies of people when they die, or at least having one's own body still being useful. Can't you see how wonderful it is? There are so many parts that can be reused as furniture, and it's a waste to throw them away . . . isn't that more sacrilegious?"

"No, it isn't," Naoki retorted. "What's wrong with everyone? It's crazy. Look at this!" he said, ripping out his necktie pin and throwing it to the floor. "It's made from fingernails pulled from someone's body. A *dead* body! It's grotesque. Horrifying!"

"Stop! Don't break it! If you hate it so much, why do you wear it?"

"It's an engagement gift from my boss. It's revolting—even just touching it makes my skin crawl."

I held back my tears and yelled, "It's not like using human material is uncivilized. It's far more heartless to just burn it all!"

"That's enough!"

We always ended up fighting over this issue. I couldn't for the life of me understand why Naoki was so averse to wearing or using anything human.

"I'm sorry," I said. "I'll throw it away." I took off the sleek black sweater and, stifling my sobs, scrunched it up and stuffed it into the kitchen garbage can. As I stood there in my silk undershirt feeling miserable, I felt Naoki put his arms around me from behind.

"I'm sorry I got so emotional. I don't think I'll ever be able to make you understand, but somehow I find human hair sweaters and bone cutlery and furniture terrifying."

Naoki's slim arms rubbed gently against me. His body was enveloped in a soft cashmere cardigan. I couldn't understand why he thought human hair was so wrong when goat hair was fine. But I noticed his hands were trembling slightly and said in a small voice, "I'm sorry, I was wrong—especially since I knew you didn't like it."

"No. I'm wrong for making you put up with me," he murmured weakly, burying his face in my shoulder. "I just can't understand why everyone is okay with something so barbaric. Cats or dogs or rabbits would never do anything like this. Normal animals don't make sweaters or lamps out of the dead bodies of their fellow creatures. I just want to be like other animals and do what's right . . ."

I couldn't think of anything to say to that, and gently stroked the cashmere-enveloped arms that clung to me. Turning to face him, I hugged his hunched-over body to me and rubbed his back. He relaxed a little and sighed, his cold lips touching my neck. With his face buried in my neck, I kept on stroking his backbone for the longest time.

When I told Miho that I'd decided I wouldn't consider any furnishings made from human material, her eyes widened.

"No way! You're telling me that even with your budget, you're not going to buy the shinbone chair or the rib-cage table or the finger bone clock or the dried stomach lampshade?"

"Nope."

"Not even the display cabinet of teeth strung together? The warm rug made with human hair?"

"No. I don't want Naoki to suffer. Our house should be somewhere we can both feel comfortable."

Frowning, Miho closed the catalogs she'd spread out in front of me. "I wish I didn't have to say this," she said in a low voice, "but don't you think Naoki's sick? How come he's so neurotic about human materials?"

"I don't know. It's probably got something to do with having had a bad relationship with his father when he was little."

"He ought to get some counseling. It's abnormal. In any case, one day we'll all be turned into sweaters or clocks or lamps when we die. We humans are also materials—and that's wonderful!"

Miho was right, but I shook my head. "I agree with you, but . . . anyway, for now I intend to furnish our house in a way that won't cause any distress for Naoki."

Miho finally seemed to understand that I wasn't going to budge, and she sighed. "Okay, okay. But it's such a waste when, with your budget, you could get some fabulous furniture. Oh well, I guess we'll go with this dining table and chairs that don't have any human bone in them."

"Thanks."

"I really recommend that chandelier with scales made from human nails for your living room, but I suppose we're going to have to settle for this glass one."

"Yes, if I may."

Sighing, Miho went on sticking Post-it notes in the catalog as we decided on each item.

"I wonder why other animals don't reuse the bodies of their own dead," I said.

"Beats me. But the female praying mantis eats the male, doesn't she? It totally makes sense. I think there are some animals that know to make good use of their dead."

"Really? I guess . . ."

"Nana, aren't you being poisoned by Naoki?"

"Of course not. But I don't really understand what he means by 'barbaric.' That's what he says about using human products. But I think it's more barbaric to burn everything without reusing the materials. We use the same word to condemn each other's values. I wonder if we can really carry on like this . . ."

"Well, I really couldn't say. But Nana, you're doing your best to understand him, aren't you? If you're willing to make mutual concessions, you'll definitely be able to work things out together," she said warmly, and I gave a sigh of relief.

"Okay then," she said. "I'll draw up the invoice on these items and place the orders. It'll take a while, so feel free to look around."

"Thanks."

Miho picked up the catalogs with the Post-it notes and went to the back of the store. I gazed absently around. Time flowed by at a leisurely pace here, maybe because it was afternoon, with happy-looking young couples and genteel elderly ladies all browsing around the furniture. The first floor was full of cheap plastic and glass furnishings, but the second floor had quality furniture on display. Even the armrests of the couch I was now sitting on were of white bone.

There were some bowls made from inverted craniums on a row of dining tables at the other side of the store.

Hanging from the ceiling was one of the chandeliers with human nail scales that Miho had recommended. Warm light, somewhere between pink and yellow, filtered out through the nails. How happy I would be sitting down to a special dinner with Naoki beneath such a chandelier, with soup in those skull dishes on the table!

I glanced down at my own nails. They looked identical to the ones on the chandelier. After I died, how lovely it would be to have them made into such a beautiful chandelier for someone to enjoy. However much I made a show of going along with Naoki, I would never stop caring for my body, knowing it would someday be converted into furnishings. I would always feel that I too was a material, that I would continue to be put to practical use after I died. The thought that this was a marvelous and noble process was deeply rooted within me.

I stood up and went over to a nearby bookcase. The dividers were made of bone, probably shoulder blades, given their size. There were several real books placed on the shelves to model what it would look like in the home. Naoki liked books, and I thought how perfect his study would be with such a splendid bookcase in it. I picked up a small dictionary that was leaning against the divider and looked up the word *barbaric*, which had been niggling me for a while.

Ruthless, merciless, savage, heinous.

But I could only think that this applied more to Naoki's idea of burning people's bodies when they died. He was such a gentle person and I still couldn't believe he could be so harsh and cruel as to say that we should discard the entire body even though so much could be reused.

But I loved him. For his sake, I was resolved to spend the rest of my life without wearing or using human material, without touching the people who, after their deaths, continued to surround us with their warmth as material and furnishings.

The following Sunday, Naoki and I went to visit his family in Yokohama.

We had already completed the formalities for our engagement, and now there were all kinds of matters to discuss, like what time to hold the ceremony, whom to invite, and so forth. Naoki's little sister was going to be in charge of receiving guests on the groom's side, so we had to talk about that, too.

Naoki's father had died five years previously. His mother and sister welcomed us cheerfully.

"Come on in! Sorry to take up your time when you're so busy."

"Not at all! Lovely to see you."

Naoki's sister Mami was a graduate student some years younger than him, and had treated me affectionately ever since he and I had started dating.

"I'm so happy you're going to be my elder sister, Nana," she said delightedly as she served us homemade brownies.

Their mother poured tea to go with Mami's treats, and we chatted while enjoying them.

"Naoki, why don't you play the trumpet at the wedding? Wouldn't it be a great way to show your love for Nana?" Mami asked.

"No way! It's years since I've played any music, and I'd be far too self-conscious now. Out of the question."

Naoki looked really cute with his embarrassed smile, and I snuggled up to him happily, feeling that it had been ages since I'd seen him looking so calm and relaxed.

After we'd been talking for a while, Naoki's mother stood up, saying, "I've got something for the two of you."

She went into another room and came back with a long, thin wooden box. She put it on the table and gently opened the lid. Wondering what it was, I peered inside to see what looked like some thin washi paper.

"What is it?" We both looked at her questioningly.

"It's a veil made from your father," she informed us in hushed voice, gazing at it as she took the diaphanous fabric out of the box. It was indeed a billowy, floaty veil made from human skin.

"Five years ago, when your father got cancer, it was his dying wish to be made into a veil. It must have been just around the time you started dating Nana, Naoki. He always was too strict with you, so it was hardly surprising that you rebelled against him. You never did make up after that quarrel ended in fisticuffs when he tried to force

14

you into medical college. He used to say he'd as good as disowned you, and he refused to talk about you. But then, right at the end, he said, 'The boy's a fool, but he's got taste in women,' and he told me he wanted to be made into a veil for the wedding ceremony."

"Ah . . ."

I sneaked a quick look at Naoki. He was staring at the veil, his face utterly expressionless.

"You didn't come to the funeral, so I never had the chance to tell you about it, but I always believed this day would come. Naoki, please forgive your father. Use this veil for your wedding.

"Nana, why don't you try it on?" Mami begged me, her eyes red and filled with tears. "Isn't it magnificent?"

Gingerly I reached out and touched the veil. Human skin was generally considered too flimsy and delicate for garments. It looked like rough Japanese washi paper, but it was supersoft to the touch.

"Nana, look this way."

My mother-in-law gently lifted the veil and put it over my head, fixing it with a small comb, so that my upper body was enveloped in its lightness.

The veil reached down to my lower back, covering my ears, cheeks, and shoulders in my father-in-law's soft skin. It was plain and extremely simple, but if I looked closely, I could see the fine lines of the distinctive mesh of his skin, like delicate lacework. I felt as though I were swathed in an infinite number of particles of light residing in each individual cell.

"It looks amazing on you, Nana!"

My mother-in-law and Mami both looked enthralled.

Faint spots and moles left on my father-in-law's skin formed an intricate pattern, and here and there in the light, the white and yellowish-brown blended to give a bluish tinge, complex hues intertwining in a way that could never be manufactured artificially. The rays of sun shining in through the window were softened by the veil as they gently filtered through and coalesced on my skin.

With my whole body swathed in the skin-tinged glow, I felt as though I were standing in the most sacred church in the world.

I looked at Naoki through the delicate, beautiful veil. Still looking down, he slowly raised his arm and lifted the hem. I half expected him to rip it off, but he murmured in a low voice, "This scar . . . That was the one from junior high . . ."

Next to his hand, I saw a small mark in the lacy hem.

"That's right. It's from that time you hit him," his mother said. "It left a scar on his back, you know. I don't suppose you ever knew it, but whenever he went to a hot spring, he would proudly show it off and say, 'The boy had backbone after all.'"

Naoki stared at the veil, his expression unreadable. I watched him with bated breath, thinking he might suddenly blow up, the way he did that time he threw away his tiepin. But he kept staring at the veil, saying nothing.

After a while his pale face moved slowly toward me, as though he were falling into my father-in-law's skin.

"Dad . . ." he muttered hoarsely, burying his face in the veil.

"Naoki!" Mami exclaimed tearfully.

"Son, you forgive him, don't you?" his mother said, her voice full of emotion.

"Yes . . . of course. We'll use the veil at our wedding. Won't we, Nana?"

I wasn't sure whether I should smile or not, and just managed a weak nod. The veil trembled and softly tickled my cheeks and back with the movement. The membrane of light passing through my father-in-law's skin shimmered over my body.

In the car on the way home, I drove while Naoki slumped vacantly in the passenger seat. Despite the cold, he had the window wide open and was gazing outside.

"Hey, are we really going to use that veil?" I asked him as the box rattled on the back seat.

Naoki didn't answer, but leaned on the open window and lightly shut his eyes, snuggling in the breeze like a child who'd fallen asleep in bed.

"If you really don't want to use it," I went on patiently, choosing my words carefully, "we can always find an excuse, like the wedding planner objected to it, or it didn't go with the dress."

Naoki still didn't respond, but just sat there as the breeze messed up his hair and clothes. Irritated, I said more forcefully, "Come on, Naoki, answer me! Which is it? Were you being honest or lying for the sake of your family? Look, if you really do feel moved by your father's wishes, then we'll use it, but if you feel using human skin is too barbaric, we won't. I don't mind either way, so it's up to you to say how you feel . . .

"Which is it? Come on, tell me. Are you moved, or not? Do you think it's barbaric or not?" I demanded, raising my voice.

"I just don't know what to think anymore," he finally said. "Maybe everyone's right, and making things out of people after they die really is a wonderful, moving thing to do . . ."

I frowned, and put my foot down on the accelerator, speeding up. "Look, only you can decide whether you're moved by the idea or not, Naoki. I'm sure I don't know."

"I can't . . . I don't . . . I really don't know what to think anymore. Until this morning I was confident about how to use words like *barbaric* and *moved*, but now it all feels so groundless," he muttered vacantly. He looked like a half-wit, with his mouth hanging stupidly open, almost as if he were drooling.

"That word *barbaric* has been standing in judgment over us, though, hasn't it? Where has its power gone?"

"I don't know how I could have been so confident of myself . . . but one thing I can say is that the veil did look lovely on you. And that's because it's someone's skin. Human skin really does suit people."

Naoki shut his mouth and said no more.

The only sounds in the car were from the breeze and the veil's box rattling on the back seat.

A hundred years later, what would our bodies be used for? Would we be chair legs or sweaters or clock hands? Would we be used for a longer time after our deaths than the time we'd been alive?

Naoki was leaning back in the seat, his arms hanging limply, as if he'd become a material object. The breeze was ruffling his hair and eyelashes. Beneath his sideburns, there was a slight scar where he'd once cut himself shaving. That scar would probably still be there if he ever became a lampshade or a book cover one day, I mused.

Quietly taking one hand off the steering wheel, I took his hand, which was lying there, abandoned. It was warm, and he squeezed mine back. The sensation of his skin against mine was similar to the way I'd felt earlier, enveloped in the veil. The faint wriggle of finger bones and the pulsing of veins beneath his skin were conveyed through my fingertips.

Right now the live Naoki, not yet converted into a material, was holding my hand. We were spending our very short time as living beings sharing our body heat. Feeling this life was a precious momentary illusion, I squeezed his slim fingers even tighter.

A Magnificent Spread

It was Sunday morning, and my husband and I were having breakfast.

We bought all our meals via the online store Happy Future Foods, which sold everything from soup with cubed frozen vegetables to Future Oatmeal and freeze-dried bread and salad. Facing each other across the table, we put a variety of products reminiscent of space food into our mouths.

Happy Future Foods had the slogan "We deliver food for the next generation to your dining table" and was touted as being popular with celebrities in other countries. My husband was completely sold on the store, and nowadays practically all the food on our table came from there.

Most of it was either frozen or freeze-dried, which saved us the trouble of cooking it, but it was expensive, so we ended up spending a lot. As I put the green-colored Future Oatmeal into my mouth, I thought I'd better brush my teeth with whitening powder straight after eating.

My smartphone rang, and I peered at the screen to see that it was my little sister. I answered the call and went to sit on the sofa.

"What's up, Kumi? It's not like you to call so early."

"Are you free on the first Sunday of next month?" she asked, speaking unusually fast. "My fiancé's parents are coming over for lunch that day."

"*What?*" I was speechless. I hadn't even known that she had a boyfriend!

"It's the first time I'm meeting them, and I'm supposed to be cooking some dishes from home for them."

"Eh? You don't mean . . ."

"So I want you to come and help me. Please?"

"When you say dishes from home, Kumi, do you mean—"

"We'll do lunch with my parents another time, so this time it'll be just my boyfriend and his parents, you and me, and I want to prepare food for the five of us. You'll help, won't you? Please? I'll be back in touch when the details are settled," she said, and hung up.

"Was that Kumi?" asked my husband, who was sitting at the table eating his Future Oatmeal. "What was she saying?"

"She says she's going to meet her fiancé's parents."

"Wow! Big news!"

He was drinking a Happy Future diet drink with his meal. It was all the rage lately, a complete health drink that meant you didn't need to take any other supplements. It consisted of a pale blue powder that you mixed into carbonated water, and contained a bacterium developed by NASA that would supposedly rejuvenate you and give you a muscular body.

"So Kumi's getting married! Well, she is almost thirty, after all, just about the right age." He looked really happy.

I put my phone down on the table and told him, "And she says she is going to cook some dishes from home for them."

"What? No way!!" My husband's face turned white, and he shot to his feet, still holding his drink. "No, no, she mustn't do that. This is a serious occasion!"

"That's what she said, and you know she won't budge an inch if she's made a decision."

"Yes, I know, but her whole life could be affected by this meeting!"

He looked so furious that I sighed and said, "I guess . . . well, we'll just have to try to change her mind before then, won't we . . ."

Kumi was three years younger than me, and she'd been in junior high when she suddenly announced, "In my previous life, I was a kind of warrior in the magical city of Dundilas."

"You were?" I was in senior high school by then, and I just listened quietly without contradicting her.

"Now I'm living in Japan as the child of ordinary parents," she said, "but in the magical city of Dundilas I had supernatural powers, which I used on missions fighting enemies. I've been reborn temporarily in this body. I'm just borrowing it for now, and once it comes to the end of its life, I intend to go back home."

"Is that so?"

She apparently had quite a complex setup in her mind, and every now and then she would tell me all kinds of things about her previous life. I didn't actually dislike hearing her talk about it.

"I am grateful to this family for caring for me, but sometimes I really miss the world of my former life," she would occasionally say, her voice sad. At those times, she looked like she might actually go back to wherever Dundilas was. From her perspective, the people of her former life were her real family, and my parents and I were probably more like strangers to her.

"I suppose you do."

I always listened to her sympathetically.

"You should have stopped her right there," my mother grumbled. By then Kumi had already started telling some of her close friends at school about her previous life, and rumors about her had spread throughout the school.

I thought she'd probably get over it when she went to senior high school, but lots of her friends from junior high went on to the same school and she'd been in too deep to back out. Her graduation album was full of messages saying things like, "Take me with you to the magical city sometime, okay?" and "Keep fighting those enemies!"

She'll have to stop when she goes to university, my mother said, but I wasn't so sure. And as I'd thought, when some friends from her club came over, I overheard them in her room talking about her magical world.

"Kumi, you're a master of the dark forces, after all."

"Yep. Don't tell anyone, though."

Around that time, a friend told me about "adolescent delusion syndrome." I was impressed that there was a name for my sister's phenomenon, but it was only a slang term and not an officially recognized illness.

And so Kumi entered adulthood still behaving like someone with superpowers.

Watching her as she grew up, never giving an inch about her other life, I couldn't help feeling some kind of respect for her. I began to think that the coarse slang term didn't apply to her after all. She was more serious than that, and it wasn't just a passing phase.

She went to work for a company where she was the only new graduate among middle-aged men, and they indulged her strange pronouncements with affectionate comments—"You're a funny one, Kumi-chan." Normally someone like her would be made fun of or ostracized, but somehow she was blessed with people who understood her. She didn't have many friends, but there were always some at her side who listened to her stories about the magical city of Dundilas without ever making fun of her.

My mother didn't understand her at all and tried to make her stop fantasizing by yelling at her, and I often had to intervene to protect my sister. They didn't get on at all well, and after graduating from university, Kumi left home and started living alone.

It was around that time when she started eating weird things. She began cooking for herself, saying she was making food from the magical city of Dundilas. Whenever she went out, she would eat normal things, such as curry or steak, but at home she apparently always ate her special food.

Kumi and I were both born and bred in the humdrum suburbs of Saitama, and I don't know why she turned out this way. Still, as long as she was happy, I didn't have any problem with it.

I had never eaten her food from the magical city of Dundilas, though. I liked hearing her stories, but I found the food she was eating downright scary. I couldn't summon the courage to put such weird-looking food into my body. And if I, who understood my sister's world quite well, couldn't eat it, then the idea of serving this food to her fiancé's parents was hardly advisable. As my husband had made clear, we had to stop Kumi from carrying out this plan.

"You're old enough to know better, Kumi," Mom screeched. "Just stop it!"

I grimaced. The three of us were having dinner together at an Italian restaurant. Mom and I had waited outside Kumi's office and managed to grab her as she left work to bring her here.

"It's all very well saying stop . . . but stop what?" she asked.

Mom was getting emotional, but Kumi kept her cool. What Mom seemed to be saying was that Kumi should be cured of being herself, which I agreed was over the top.

"I don't think there's any particular need for you to change, Kumi," I told her honestly. "But I do think making other people eat your food is problematic. Even if some people understand your magical city of Dundilas, eating the food you make is another matter. It's not like it's exactly believable."

"What do you mean, believable?" She looked at me calmly, aware that I was more likely to understand her than Mom was.

"When you eat the food someone makes for you, it means you believe in the world they live in, right? Even if people have fun hearing about your world, putting it into their mouth is another matter. I think food is all weird anyway, so there's no way I can eat it unless I believe in it." I pointed at the plate of pasta in front of me. "For example, this pasta with peach and coriander—since it's made in a restaurant like this by a respectable chef, I can delight in eating it. If one of the local elementary school kids brought it in a Tupperware box, though, I'd probably think pasta with peach sounded disgusting and wouldn't be able to eat it. It's only when we believe in the person who makes it that we're able to put weird stuff in our mouth."

"You're so matter-of-fact, aren't you?" Kumi said to me.

"Maybe I am."

The Happy Future Food that my husband and I ate wasn't all that different from the magical city of Dundilas food. But the company at least made a good effort to be credible. I believed that eating meant being brainwashed by the particular world of the food, and I just couldn't bring myself to ingest food from my sister's unstable, fictitious world.

"Has your fiancé eaten your food, Kumi?"

"Keiichi? No, he hasn't. He's seen it, but he said there's no way he could eat it."

"You *see*?" Mom shouted. Mom being so emotional really wasn't helping, I thought.

"Of course, the instinct to eat food that is safe is hard-wired in us," I told Kumi. "So what you have to do is try to convince everyone that your food is safe and that it's wonderful too, even if it means lying. If you can manage that, I think I'd be able to eat it."

"I understand what you're saying, but I don't think it's possible. I'm pretty sure I'm the only one who truly believes in the magical city of Dundilas."

I nodded, grateful that she was being so levelheaded. "Well, that's true, I guess. So how about cooking something appropriate and safe, like curry or hamburger."

"Because my boyfriend wants me to cook my food for them."

"Eh?" I blurted out. "Are you serious? It was his idea?"

"It's not like I offered, you know. I only ever eat food from the magical city of Dundilas at home. It's just that Keiichi insisted."

"Even though he won't eat it? But why would he want you to cook it?"

She shrugged. "No idea. Maybe he wants us to split up."

I tilted my head doubtfully. Thinking that my sister's fiancé sounded like a nutjob, I stuck my fork into a bit of peach and pasta.

When I got home, my husband was making his usual drink, mixing the blue powder in a glass of sparkling water.

"Hi there!" I called. "Is that all you're having for dinner today, too?"

"Yeah. It's amazing, this stuff. Ever since I started drinking it, my body feels so light."

"I see."

I disliked the way the drink smelled of shampoo, so I'd never actually tried it. And what's more, a month's supply cost twenty thousand yen. One of us drinking it was enough.

"How was Kumi?"

I threw my bag down on the sofa and sighed. "Um, it looks like we're going to be preparing that weird food of hers."

"Really? Well, I guess she's finished then," he said flatly.

I looked at him in surprise. "What do you mean?"

"I mean, the engagement will probably be called off. She's finished." He even looked a little happy as he drank his blue drink. "What a waste, though. Just when she had the chance to lead a normal life. I told my colleagues at work about her, and they all laughed."

"Really," I said, for lack of anything better, and opened the fridge to get some water to drink. Inside were rows of Happy Future Food in packs. I took out some mineral water and drank it. What on earth was so different about my husband and my sister, I wondered.

So was there no hope for my sister? Probably not, from a conventional point of view. The reason my husband was so obsessed with eating Happy Future Foods was that he thought it was food for successful people. He was ingesting a fragment of a wonderful lifestyle.

I found that side of my husband amusing. The more expensive something was, the more he was taken in by it. I'd heard that a scam was more effective if the scammer asked for a million yen rather than a hundred yen, and looking at my husband, I had to conclude it was true. A yearning for "a higher level of living" was what made my husband drink that blue concoction. The pressure on our household budget was a concern, but for some reason I felt refreshed to see him happily drink it down.

The way my husband trusted the world and played up to it felt somehow pure to me. That was probably what I liked about him and why I married him.

The Sunday my sister was to cook for her boyfriend's parents was a cloudless, bright day.

Her apartment was small, just one room, and our parents' place was too far away, so it was decided that we would hold the party in my house.

"I'm so sorry," she said, embarrassed. "Not only did I rope you into helping, but I even borrowed your place!"

I quickly answered, "No problem at all, don't worry about it." I was curious to see how her boyfriend's parents would react.

My husband was out for the day at some sort of conference involving different businesses. It was probably just an excuse to get out of eating my sister's weird food.

Kumi came over early in the morning, carrying bags full of provisions.

"Dandelions, fish mint . . . is this what we're eating today?"

"Yep. The setting is medicinal herbs that grow in the magical realm."

"What's in this can?"

"That's the setting of food sold on the black market in the underground arcade in the magical world."

All my sister's food had a setting, and even though I didn't want to taste any of it, I was amused to see how she was always quick to elaborate.

"Look, are you sure it shouldn't be proper food?"

She shot me a look. "What do you mean, proper food?"

"Like dishes with a name, spareribs or chicken stew or something."

"So anything with a name is like proper food?"

"A name puts whoever's eating it at ease, doesn't it? Even a con man always gives his name."

"Your theories are always too weird to be of help," she said with a sigh.

"All right, then . . . anyway, let's get going. Where shall I start?"

"First I want you to boil the dandelion flowers. See that orange juice over there? Bring that to the boil and put them in it."

"Okay."

My sister deftly got on with the cooking. She shredded the fish mint, put it into some flour, added some water, and mixed it up.

"What's that?"

"The main dish."

"Does fish mint grow in the magical city of Dundilas?"

"Yeah, lots of it."

If she said so, then it must be true, I thought. I did as she said and emptied the dandelions out of the bag.

Just after noon, my sister's fiancé and his parents rang the doorbell.

"My name is Keiichi Sawaguchi, Kumi's fiancé. Pleased to meet you."

It was the first time I'd met Kumi's boyfriend, and he seemed pleasant, not at all the type of weirdo who would purposely get someone to cook dishes from the magical city of Dundilas.

"We're so sorry for imposing on you today."

His parents, too, were elegant and mild-mannered. His mother, Sachie, looked easy to get along with, her eyes crinkling at the corners when she smiled, and his father, Eiji, looked strong and rugged, but his manner of bowing was charmingly shy.

"This is my girlfriend, Kumi," Keiichi said to his parents.

"Pleased to meet you," Kumi said, bowing her head.

"I'm Kumi's sister. Thank you for coming all the way here," I said to them, bowing deeply at her side. "I'm afraid our apartment is a little cramped, but please do come in. My sister's cooking is very simple, but we hope you will enjoy it."

The Sawaguchis smiled. "Thank you."

Sachie and Eiji sat on the far side of the table, with Kumi and Keiichi sitting opposite them. There weren't enough chairs at the living room table, so I brought my husband's work chair from his study.

After a short rest, Kumi and I went to the kitchen and brought the first dish to the table.

"What is this?" Sachie asked, peering curiously at it.

"The main dish, apparently," I explained vaguely. "I'm not sure it'll be to your taste, so please don't force yourself to eat it . . . um, I have some barley tea ready here to wash it down with. Here are some tissues and some sick bags."

"You sure are well prepared!" said Keiichi, smiling.

"And this?"

"Dandelion stems braided and simmered in orange juice. Underneath are meatballs stuffed with dandelion flowers."

"Ah . . ."

Stories were fundamental to my sister's cooking, more important than the flavor. She had told me all about this while we were cooking. The orange juice apparently represented the blood of a primitive monster, while the ground pork imitated synthetic meat sold on the black market in underground malls in the magical city of Dundilas. Dandelions grew profusely in the forests of the magical realm, and she'd often eaten them in her previous life.

I understood the images, but I couldn't help thinking that as food, it looked pretty disgusting. Apart from anything, I had no idea where she had actually picked the dandelions and fish mint. If she'd picked them in the neighborhood, they must be covered in exhaust fumes.

It seemed the Sawaguchis felt the same way, for they just smiled without making any move to help themselves.

"Um, may I offer you something from our house too?" I said, unable to bear it any longer. "I don't know whether it will be to your taste either, but you may want a break from such exotic food."

"Well, er . . . um, thank you." Sachie looked at me in evident relief. Perhaps she was not very good at maintaining appearances.

"Having said that, I haven't prepared anything special, and only have things we always eat at home . . ."

"No problem."

But their happy expressions clouded when I brought some Happy Future Foods to the table.

"Er . . . what is it?"

"Happy Future Food. It's really good for you and has an antioxidant effect. It's extremely popular abroad, so we buy it online."

"I see . . ."

I laid out some cubes made from freeze-dried vegetables and some fruits powder salad with bright blue dressing. I'd selected items I'd thought were not too off-putting, but the Sawaguchis looked quite taken aback.

"Um, I don't suppose there's any plain steamed rice, is there?" Eiji asked timidly.

"Not white rice, but I do have some artificial rice made from a powder filled with antioxidants. Although it is a bit sour and something of an acquired taste . . ." I said, showing them the green artificial rice in a Tupperware box.

"Er . . . never mind," Sachie muttered.

"Come to think of it, dear, you have some of those snacks with you, don't you?" Eiji said, suddenly remembering.

"Oh, yes, you're right!" Sachie nodded. "When Keiichi told us about this lunch, I got the impression that you liked unusual food. I guess I got the wrong end of the hook . . . but anyway, this is from the countryside round our way. I hope you'll like it," she said, taking out a paper bag containing various containers stuffed with grubs stewed in soy sauce and syrup. One jar contained what looked like small white caterpillars, and another jar held something similar but a little larger. Plus a plastic box containing what appeared to be grasshoppers.

There were so many delicious foods from the countryside, so why on earth did she have to bring three types of stewed bugs? I didn't want to put them in my mouth, so I looked at my sister, who was sitting next to me. She apparently felt the same way, as there was an undisguised look of disgust on her face.

"Um . . . I'm afraid I'm not keen on sweet stewed things," I said. "Er, I must say I prefer savory dishes . . ."

"Really?" Sachie said, looking disappointed. "They do taste good with rice, though . . ."

"They make an especially good snack to go with sake," Eiji added.

"Ah . . ."

The spread on the table now included the dishes from the magical city of Dundilas, the high-quality pouches of Happy Future Food, and the various insects.

I really didn't want to eat anything I didn't normally eat, and I looked around at everybody's faces to see that they all seemed to feel the same way and were sitting expressionlessly, drinking barley tea without making any move to eat.

"You *see?*" Keiichi said suddenly.

"Huh?"

"What do you mean?"

Everyone looked bewildered, but Keiichi ignored them and went on. "This is exactly what I wanted to see today."

I had no idea what he was talking about and looked at my sister for help, but she too was staring at him open-mouthed, apparently not understanding anything either.

"Everyone thinks the food other people eat is disgusting, and they refuse to eat it. And that's the way it should be, as far as I'm concerned."

"What are you talking about?" I asked.

Keiichi launched into a rant, gesticulating wildly. "What people eat is part of their own culture. It's the culmination of their own unique personal life experiences. And it's wrong to force it on other people."

"Ah . . ." I said, pushing my chair back to avoid being hit by his long arms, which he was waving around as he talked.

"Even if I marry Kumi, I have no intention of eating her cooking. And there is absolutely no need for her to eat or cook the food that I or my parents eat. We each have our own cultures to live. There is no need whatsoever for us to cater to each other or merge into each other."

Sachie frowned. "You might well say that," she said, "but if you keep on eating like you do now, you're not going to live very long."

"That's my business, and the decision is mine alone."

I couldn't help asking, "Er, so what do you eat, Keiichi?"

"Keiichi eats only sweets and potato fries," my sister said.

Keiichi nodded emphatically. "Ever since I was a child," he said.

"Really? Wow." He was quite tall, and I was impressed that he could have grown so well on such an unbalanced diet.

"I love sweets and potato fries. If I have my own way, that's all I'll eat my whole life. I once lived with a fiancée, but it didn't last long. She tried to force me to eat the same things as she did. Even though we had different cultures, she tried to disrupt my life as if that were normal. Even though we each had our own cultures! We argued every day and eventually split up."

"I see."

"I think it's great that Kumi has her own independent eating habits. She never caters to anyone else. Nor does she try to impose her culture on anyone else. I think we can live happily together, with her eating what she wants to eat and me eating what I want to eat."

"I guess that makes sense." I was beginning to understand why Keiichi and my sister were drawn to each other.

"As a couple, Kumi and I will never eat what the other has cooked. And I want you to realize this too, Mom and Dad. In our house, if I'm eating chocolate cookies and pizza potato chips and Kumi's eating her food from the magical city of Dundilas, it doesn't mean that we're not getting along. On the contrary, it's because we love each other's cultures. And if we visit you in the countryside at New Year's or in the summer for Obon, I don't want you forcing your food on her. Our eating habits are dear to us, and I want you to respect them and not interfere—"

Eiji had been listening to this lecture, frowning, but now he interrupted. "But look, Keiichi. Marriage is about two families coming together. It's about continuing the culture of those families, isn't it?"

Sachie restrained him. "That's enough, dear. It's what Keiichi wants. Deep down, I was hoping that your wife would carry on the food traditions of the Sawaguchi family, but I suppose that was quite arrogant . . ."

"Oh, really!"

Eiji glared at Sachie, but she continued quietly. "I mean, just look at this lunch table. It's hell on earth! It's all over the place. Until I got married, I'd always thought bugs were gross and it was normal to kill them and throw them away. I'd always thought bugs were garbage, but when I married into the Sawaguchi family, I was forced to eat them. When I think about that, *everything* on this table is garbage—all of it."

"Sachie . . ."

"I don't at all think I was wrong in carrying on your family's traditions, dear, but just look at the wretched state of this lunch table! It's not like in the old days, you know. Nowadays people will gladly tuck into all sorts of strange things. And if we merge our traditions with new ones like this, the food is only going to get creepier."

"Yes, Mom, that's exactly what I mean," Keiichi said happily. "We don't have to eat out of the same pot to understand each other."

"You think?" Eiji seemed to have more to say, but seeing the disastrous state of the table, he appeared to resign himself to the situation. "I guess our ideas are obsolete now," he muttered. "And even if Kumi did carry on our family's traditions, maybe it doesn't really matter when you'll only eat sweets or potato fries anyway . . ."

"Right!" Keiichi shouted.

"I agree!" I couldn't help shouting. "I think eating something is a matter of trusting the world that produced it. But there's also sincerity in not trusting something and refusing it. I myself wouldn't eat these products if my husband didn't buy them. They're weird colors, they feel like plastic on the tongue, and they smell like air freshener. Garbage, as you put it. But I like the way my husband feels about eating them, so I end up just going along with him."

"I see . . ."

"How about a toast?" Keiichi shouted excitedly. "Here's to all our uniquely disgusting food!"

My sister nodded enthusiastically and stood up, saying, "I'll go get you some french fries from McDonald's!"

Keiichi stopped her. "No, don't bother. I've got some Pringles, macadamia nut chocolate, and Pepsi in my bag. That'll do for me."

"That's just like you to be eating that sort of thing, Keiichi," said Sachie. "We always struggled with your eating problem ever since you were little. But I suppose that's who you are."

Everyone seemed strangely excited, babbling away and not making much sense. But I felt some kind of emotional harmony prevailing, and I went to get some beer from the refrigerator.

"Well then, everyone, how about some beer? There's also mineral water and a Happy Future Foods drink for anyone who doesn't want alcohol."

"I'll have a beer," said Eiji.

"Mineral water for me," my sister said.

"May I have some more barley tea?" said Sachie.

Everyone took what they wanted, and we raised our glasses high.

"Well then, *kanpai!*"

"Here's to everyone's disgusting food!"

We were just getting into full swing when I heard the sound of a key in the lock. The living room door opened, and my husband poked his head in.

"I'm back . . . ah, so everyone's still here, I see. I'm sorry for barging in like this."

"Not at all," Keiichi said, bowing his head. "Please excuse us for being here."

My husband smiled and shook his hand, then sat down in the chair I'd been sitting in. I went to the refrigerator to get some of that blue drink he liked so much, and I heard him cry out, "Wow! What a magnificent spread you have here! Please do let me join you. This is the epitome of cross-cultural exchange!"

My sister came in and whispered in my ear, "What's he going on about?"

"Beats me . . ."

As we puzzled over this unexpected development, we heard him speaking eloquently.

"You know, today I've been at a conference for exchanging business ideas. I was invited to join a seminar on food. It was amazing! Life-changing! Food is an excellent means for cultural exchange. The things you can learn from each meal! And not just nutrition. When you eat, you ingest culture, too. I realized that's where the future of our alimentary lifestyle lies."

I somehow got the idea where he was coming from and whispered to my sister, "That seminar really got to him, huh? He's so gullible."

My husband had always aspired to a higher living standard, so he was easily taken in by study groups and seminars that used it as a lure. He was especially susceptible to expensive things, so I was sure he must have paid a high fee for the seminar.

"Look, there are three hundred and sixty-five days in the year," he went on in a rapturous tone, "and at three meals a day that makes a total of one thousand and ninety-five meals. Every single one of them is an opportunity, you know. You keep learning about different cultures through those meals, and that's the key to being successful in life. People who always eat the same food are constantly missing out on the opportunity to learn, you see."

"I beg your pardon?" said Sachie, who looked completely lost.

Ignoring her, my husband picked up a small plate off the table. "Wow, this looks so delicious! The whole table is glowing! What sort of bread is this?"

Kumi jumped up and ran over to him. "Oh! That's from the magical city of Dundilas. It's—"

"Oh, you made it, Kumi? It's wonderful. May I have a piece?"

"Um, well, sure . . . but I don't know if you'll like it . . ."

"Eating things you don't like—that's what enriches our existence, Kumi," he said, and winked at her.

Kumi smiled wanly and sat down. Since my husband had taken the chair I'd been sitting in, I perched on the stool in the kitchen. I felt kind of scared to go back to the table.

"This is something I've never seen before too. Looks tasty!" he said, putting a small caterpillar on the bread from the magical city of Dundilas. He added some Happy Future Foods freeze-dried vegetables and picked up Keiichi's Pepsi.

"Look at this! A perfect fusion of cultures! The number of cultures I can learn about in this one meal!"

And with that, he folded the piece of bread in two and bit into the unholy mix.

"Urg . . ." Sachie held her handkerchief to her mouth.

In my husband's mouth, the magical city of Dundilas bread and the caterpillar and a Happy Future Food product and the Pepsi all blended together. Nausea rose up in me, and I had to look away.

Everyone had gone pale and was staring at my husband. He carried on chewing, oblivious to the consternation around him. His cheerful voice rang out, "Mmm, this is sooo good!" The sound of him chomping in the silence of the room grated on my eardrums. "What a magnificent spread! Absolutely delicious!"

We were transfixed by the monstrous sight of my husband eating.

A Summer Night's Kiss

Summer is the season for kissing. That's what her friend Kikue used to say, Yoshiko suddenly remembered as she took in the strong fragrance of the summer's night through the screen door.

Yoshiko had just turned seventy-five. She had never had sex and hadn't kissed anyone either. She had never even once had intercourse with her older husband, who had died five years earlier. Both of their daughters had been conceived by artificial insemination, and she was still a virgin when she became a mother. Both daughters were now married, and she was thoroughly enjoying living alone in the house her husband had left to her.

In all other respects she had lived an absolutely normal life, marrying, having a family, and getting old. Even so, the moment she let drop in some conversation or other that "I have never had that experience, you see," she would get a shocked reaction: "What? Why? I mean, what about your children? Eh? Artificial insemination? Why on earth would you do that?" Everyone would start nosily inquiring into the details of Yoshiko's sexual orientation and sex life, and ultimately she got fed up with this and made sure to keep quiet about it. When she said nothing, everyone treated her as an ordinary person. Yoshiko thought this kind of response from people was shallow, cruel, and arrogant.

She was just thinking it was about time to run her bath when her cell phone rang.

It was Kikue, who lived nearby.

"Hello, it's me," she said. "Won't you come over tonight? My little sister just sent me a box of peaches, and I don't know what to do with them. You were good at making that stuff, weren't you? You know, that boiled fruit thing."

"Compote?"

"That's the stuff. Come and make some. I get off work at ten, so come and meet me at the store. About an hour from now, okay?"

"Come on, you're not trying to take an elderly woman for a night stroll, are you? Not that I mind, though."

She'd come to know Kikue, who was the same age as she was, in a club at the local community center. Kikue had this wayward side to her that Yoshiko didn't dislike. She had remained single her whole life, and after retiring from her job she'd been living off her pension and the wages from her part-time job at the local convenience store. Yoshiko had been taken aback by her working a night shift where she had to briskly carry around heavy cardboard boxes, but Kikue coolly boasted, "I grew up on a farm, so this is nothing. It just takes a kind of discipline."

Yoshiko walked through the residential area to the store where Kikue worked, arriving just as Kikue was leaving.

"Don't you have a date tonight?" Yoshiko asked teasingly.

"Don't be silly. I only go on dates when it's raining. Nights as pleasant as this feel too wholesome for kissing on the street," Kikue replied primly.

Kikue had never experienced marriage, but she loved sex, and even now she was always chatting up men in the store, and she often went to bed with boys forty or fifty years younger than herself. She bragged about how even the manager was scared of her, calling her a nymphomaniac.

The two elderly women walked along the dark street together. In this residential area at night, with hardly a soul in sight, the noise of traffic echoed like the sound of waves.

Kikue took something out of the convenience store bag she was carrying. "Would you like one of these?" It was a plastic package of sweet warabimochi dumplings. "They were near the sell-by date and about to be thrown out, so I bought them. They're nicely chilled and delicious."

As she walked, she poured some molasses syrup over them and put one in her mouth.

"You know, warabimochi resemble a boy's tongue. That's why I wanted to eat them. I feel like I'm kissing someone."

"Really? Well, I don't want one then," Yoshiko said, and shrugged.

"Oh dear, I shouldn't have said that." Kikue laughed.

Despite being polar opposites, they really were very alike. When Yoshiko had confessed that she was a virgin, all Kikue said was, "Really?"

"Well, just one then," Yoshiko said, taking one. Putting it to her mouth, she tore off a soft lump with her teeth and felt a rush of satisfaction.

"Such a passionate kiss!" Kikue laughed again, and their footsteps rang out brightly in the hushed night streets.

Two's Family

Yoshiko arrived at the hospital ward to find Kikue's bed empty. She must have gone to the bathroom or something. A women's weekly magazine, headphones, and various other items were strewn across the bed. Just the same as at home, Yoshiko thought drily and started putting them away.

"Visiting again today?" asked the woman in the next bed. "Coming every day must be quite a chore."

She must be in her fifties or so, thought Yoshiko. She herself was now seventy years old, and the woman seemed quite young to her. Yoshiko smiled at her, the corners of her eyes crinkling.

"It's not like I have anything better to do. It's boring being home all alone when you're elderly."

The woman didn't look any less impressed. "That's more than most people would do. Are you sisters? It's a great comfort at times like this to have a sister you still get along well with at an advanced age."

"No, we're not sisters. But we've been living together for about forty years now, so we are family."

The woman suddenly looked confused. "Oh . . . is that so? I see . . ." she said vaguely, then clammed up and didn't speak any more.

She was probably thinking there must be some complicated family issues, or that they were an aging lesbian couple. Yoshiko couldn't be bothered to explain, so she gave her a smile and bowed, then got back to tidying up Kikue's bed.

"Oh, you're already here?" Kikue came back into the ward dragging a drip stand along with her. "It's such a pain going to the toilet. And I have to take a urine sample every damn time too," she grumbled as she lowered herself onto the bed.

"Here, some underwear and a towel," said Yoshiko. "I'll put them in this drawer for you. And you've been moaning for some time now about wanting earphones with a longer cable, haven't you? I dropped by the electronics store and got you some."

"Thanks. Sorry to put you to so much trouble," Kikue said, taking the plastic bag containing the earphones and listlessly turning on the TV. "There's nothing worth watching."

Yoshiko put a cardigan over her shoulders, catching sight of a notebook and ball pen lying by the pillow. "You've been writing again?"

"Yes, I have. I'll read it to you once it's finished."

"No thanks, it gives me the creeps. It's not like we're schoolgirls or anything." Yoshiko was frowning, but deep down she was relieved.

Just after the cancer had been discovered, Kikue had grown quite haggard and, between tests, had started writing her will in her notebook. Yoshiko kept telling her to stop being so gloomy, but she wouldn't listen.

Kikue had always been in the habit of keeping a diary and composing poems when she felt down. But the will was the most depressing thing she'd ever written.

Then she'd learned that she could be cured by an operation, and, her spirits clearly lifted, she started writing trashy poems to pass the time. She'd once shown them to Yoshiko, but they all appeared to be about her sex life, although it wasn't clear whether she was making fun of herself or being serious when she wrote lines like, "My wrinkled fingers traced the lines of your bones beneath your shirt before undoing the white buttons" and "I put on my reading glasses and looked up at you, to see your watery pitch-black eyes gazing down on me."

"Do you mind if I go to take my bath?" Kikue asked. "I'm sorry to go when you've only just arrived, but I reserved the bath for this time."

"Sure, no problem. I'll read a book or something while I'm waiting for you. Are you okay going alone?"

"Don't be silly, I'm not that weak," Kikue said with a frown. She called the nurse to remove the drip, picked up a change of clothes and a towel, and left the ward again.

Yoshiko and Kikue had been classmates in high school. They had made a promise to each other that if they hadn't married by the time they reached thirty, they'd live together. Lots of other girls said similar things, but they were the only two who actually went through with it.

With Yoshiko being too guarded and Kikue too promiscuous, it seemed unlikely that either of them would ever find a marriage partner. And so, on Yoshiko's thirtieth birthday, they had started living together.

The following year, Yoshiko was artificially inseminated with sperm she'd bought from a sperm bank, and she gave birth to their eldest daughter, followed by a second daughter the next year. Then, when they were thirty-five, Kikue gave birth to their third daughter. They bought a condo in a suburb of Chiba and lived happily as a family of five.

The children were a lot of work, but they were adorable. Yet everyone around them seemed uncomfortable with the arrangement.

"Ms. Yamazaki, um . . . you share an apartment with Ms. Kojima, don't you—Nana's mom, from class two, year two, right?" said the homeroom teacher, looking uncomfortably around the living room on a home visit. Their eldest daughter had been in the final year of elementary school at the time.

"Nana is our youngest daughter. We raise them equally, regardless of who gave birth to them."

"Ahh . . . but children are easily confused by such complicated home environments. You should simply explain to them that you are two single mothers sharing a flat together. It'll be fine! Mizuho's a bright child, she'll understand."

"No, Kikue Kojima and I are family. We are raising our children equally, as sisters. Is there anything wrong with that?"

The teacher's expression alternated between wondering whether it was her responsibility to do something about this troublesome pupil or whether she could let it slide. "Ah, well . . . I guess there are all kinds of families . . . and Mizuho's grades are good," she answered evasively.

When Yoshiko told her daughter upon her return from cram school about the teacher's visit, Mizuho replied, unperturbed, "Well she's an ordinary person, after all. Of course ordinary people are going to respond like that."

Yoshiko pressed her, concerned. "Do other people at school say things too? You should tell me if they do."

But Mizuho looked untroubled and, sounding mature beyond her years, simply said, "Mom, do you really expect society to understand? As long as we're okay with things, why should it bother us? If it does, I don't think we can carry on like this."

Yoshiko's friends had also said things to her. Are you two actually lesbians? Why don't you just come out and say that you're only sharing an apartment because you can't afford to live on your own? She could hit them! Hadn't they themselves always said they would live together if they didn't find partners in good time? She and Kikue had simply carried through on that promise. Yet hardly anyone understood this.

There were nights when she wept silently, worried that they were burdening their children with the arrangement. Kikue's self-assured attitude never wavered, however. "Having two mothers makes for a fantastic family environment, doesn't it? The children are super happy, you know," she would say, but Yoshiko knew that she sometimes secretly wrote about her fears in her notebook.

They had been encouraging and supporting each other for forty years now. The three daughters had grown up to be mutually supportive sisters. The eldest had married and had moved to Oita, in Kyushu, when her husband was transferred there for work, and now had two children. The second had moved to France and was studying to be a translator, while the youngest had gone to university in Kyoto and upon graduation had found a job in the city. Each was living happily in her own way.

When Yoshiko informed the daughters of Kikue's illness, the eldest said, "Shall I come and stay with you for a while? I'm worried about Kikue Mom of course, but I'm also worried about you." Yoshiko had replied, "It's okay. Your children are still small, so don't go out of your way. It might be cancer, but the operation will cure her. It's really just like having your appendix out, you know."

The second daughter, always a crybaby, had been ready to jump on the next plane home, so Yoshiko told her firmly that the plane ticket would cost more than the hospital charges. The youngest came on the bullet train at the weekend to see them but immediately rushed back home again.

"In the end it's just the two of is, isn't it?" Kikue had murmured faintheartedly in the hospital ward after their youngest daughter left, saying she had to catch the last train.

"But it always was, wasn't it? That's what family is. Children always leave the nest," Yoshiko said, trying to make her feel less discouraged, but Kikue had plunged into her second notebook, probably depressed by that remark.

Kikue was wildly promiscuous and had always had lovers, but when she informed her current lover (a man fifteen years her junior) that she had cancer, he'd apparently made himself scarce. This had likely depressed her even further.

"Sorry to have kept you waiting," Kikue said as she came back in, drying her hair with a towel. "Ah, that feels better! I swear I'm going crazy from boredom. Going to the hospital shop is the only entertainment I have."

"How about chatting up some charming man in the hospital? That's what you're good at, right?"

Kikue pulled a face. "Men at death's door are not my type." Then, after a moment, she added, "But there is a guy in the surgery department next to us who isn't bad-looking," and blushed.

"Now that's more like it. If he's in surgery, he should be okay, shouldn't he? How about sneaking into his ward at night?"

"I've only spoken to him a little in the lobby, and I don't know which ward he's on. Look, won't you go get me some lipstick from the shop downstairs?"

Kikue looked more cheerful as Yoshiko started drying her hair. She had always been proud of her thick black hair, but now she had a lot more gray mixed in, and it was beginning to thin on top.

"Okay. Lipstick, right?"

"Yes, please. And you know what? They've set the date for surgery. It'll be next week."

"Oh, I see . . ."

"It's on a weekday, so please don't tell the children. Especially Mizuho. She has such a strong sense of responsibility and will drop everything and come if you tell her. She frets too much, and it gets tedious."

"Okay, I won't," Yoshiko said. All of a sudden she wondered just what Kikue meant to her. If she were to lose Kikue now, what would become of her? Her parents were already dead, and the children were all following their own life paths. She was the one most affected by Kikue's hospitalization.

"Oh, and could I ask you to buy me another notebook too? I'm about to finish this one."

Kikue looked happy. Despite having seemed so depressed earlier, now she was absorbed in writing her stupid poetry.

"Oh, do stop wasting paper!" Yoshiko exclaimed loudly to dispel her feeling of melancholy.

"Want to read the latest one?" Kikue asked mischievously.

"Leave it out! Why would I want to read your cheap porno stories?"

"How do you know it won't be a poem dedicated to you?"

"Then I definitely don't want to read it."

"You're so spiteful. Oh, look!" Kikue said, pointing outside.

Yoshiko followed her gaze and saw that it was snowing.

"I'll write about this in my poem. *The hand of my family dries my wet hair, a snowy scene on the opposite bank . . .*"

"Awful," Yoshiko said as she turned off the hair dryer and gazed at the falling snow. "I wonder what our lives would have been like if we hadn't lived together."

"Hmm. We would have been the same, I guess. Talking about trivial things, saying nasty things to each other, yet still getting by in our own way."

"Yes, I suppose you're right."

Had anything developed between them as a result of their living together? Yoshiko didn't know, but if Kikue died, she had decided she would be the chief mourner at her funeral. It was absolutely clear to her that she was the one who would play that role, not any of Kikue's former lovers.

"If the snow settles, you'll have your work cut out for you shoveling a path outside the apartment."

"You're right. So hurry up and come home."

Kikue laughed. Maybe she'd heard how Yoshiko's gruff voice had broken slightly as she said this.

"I'll be home before you know it. It's *our* house after all. I can't let you get used to doing everything the way you like it while I'm away."

The snow grew heavier, painting the world white outside the window. "It's so beautiful, isn't it?" Kikue said, leaning forward like a child. In that moment, the indigo notebook slipped from her wrinkled hands and, as though slowly flapping its wings, fluttered under the bed.

The Time of
the Large Star

A little girl once moved with her papa to a small town in a country that was far, far away. Her papa told her that because of his job, they would live there from now on.

"This country is a little strange," he told her. "Nobody sleeps here."

"So what do they do at night, then?"

"It gets dark, but night doesn't exist, so you can go outside for walks anytime you like."

The girl was happy to hear this. Being able to go for walks even when it was dark sounded wonderfully grown-up to her.

"But won't I feel sleepy?"

"Here, magic sand comes flying in from the other side of the cliff. Thanks to its magic power, nobody needs to sleep."

People led a strange lifestyle in that town. When the sun rose in the sky, turning it blue, everyone would pull a face. "The Large Star has come out," they would say, and then they'd all go home. When the sun went down, and the Time of the Little Stars began, the town grew lively. The townspeople said they didn't like the Large Star. It came too close, its rays were too strong, and it was too hot and bright. In the Time of the Little Stars, the candy store and the toy store were full of children. Just as her papa had said, no matter how much time passed, the little girl never felt sleepy. She started going for walks during the Time of the Large Star, when there weren't many other people around. The candy store and the toy store were empty, but she liked this time when they were enveloped in light.

One day in the park, she met a little boy. He was sitting on a bench reading a book. "Isn't the Large Star too bright for you?" she asked.

"Not at all. I like this time the best. The town is pure white and shining."

The girl looked around and realized that indeed, the park's slide, the buildings, the road . . . everything was reflecting the Large Star's light and was all white and sparkling.

"I don't find it dazzling either," she said primly. "In the town where I used to live, we always lived in this light."

"Oh, you're from another country? Wow! Did you happen to sleep there, by any chance?"

"Yes, we did."

"That's so cool. What does it feel like to sleep?"

"I'll teach you if you like. It's easy. If you close your eyes, you'll fall asleep right away. And you can have all kinds of dreams."

The little girl and little boy sat next to each other on the bench and closed their eyes. But however long she waited, the girl didn't fall into the world of sleep the way she used to, and the boy didn't sleep either.

"It's just that you're bad at it," the girl said. "I know— let's leave the town and go far away. Then you'll be able to sleep."

The boy looked troubled. "Don't you know? Once you've lived in this town, you'll never be able to sleep again."

The girl was shocked.

"Once you're under the spell, you'll never be free of it. Grown-ups say it's convenient, but I would really like to experience what it's like to sleep."

The little girl burst into tears, and the boy desperately tried to soothe her. "Once we've grown up," she said, "let's try fainting."

"What's fainting?"

"It's just like sleeping. We both have to give ourselves a big surprise. Then we will faint together."

"I see," the boy said. "Let's try fainting together some-time, then."

The boy gave her one of the white flowers that grew in the park. It would be wonderful if she could faint with the boy, she thought, but she couldn't stop her tears. The Large Star illuminated the two of them in its pure white light.

Poochie

"Could you take over feeding duty today?" Yuki asked me.

Apparently the teacher had asked her to help with the class chores that afternoon.

"Sure," I said happily.

"Thanks," she said, looking relieved. "If we finish quickly, I'll come along too."

Yuki was super reliable and hadn't missed a single feeding duty until now. I'd gotten her to take my turn lots of times when I had a piano lesson or needed to help Mom. I was happy that for once, she'd asked me to fill in for her.

After classes ended, I ran to the mountain behind our school. There was a small hut on the mountain where Yuki and I kept our secret pet. In my bag I had three bread rolls left over from lunch.

Poochie was waiting patiently for me.

"Sorry, Poochie. Are you hungry?"

Poochie lumbered around to face me and stared fixedly through his broken glasses at the bread rolls I was holding.

I didn't know where Poochie had come from. One day Yuki had told me, "I've got a secret pet that I'm keeping up on the mountain. Do you want to come and see him, Mizuho?"

My heart pounded. Yuki was a quiet girl who never talked much about herself. She was a little different from my other classmates, seeming to live in a world of her own, and she always seemed so detached when observing us classmates and our teacher. I had a secret crush on her.

And now she'd confided a secret just to me. I was ecstatic.

So when she led a man about the same age as my dad out of the shed saying, "This is Poochie," I'd been utterly floored.

"This . . . is your pet, Yuki?"

"Yep. Cute, isn't he?"

Seeing the middle-aged man staring at the ground as Yuki stroked his head, what I felt was fear.

"Shouldn't you put a collar on him?"

My immediate response was that perhaps we should restrain this dangerous pet to make sure he couldn't do us any harm.

"I guess so," Yuki said, agreeing. "After all, he is a pet. Good thinking, Mizuho. It never even occurred to me."

Next time I went to see Poochie, he was wearing a red collar. It didn't make any sense to have a collar without a chain attached, but Yuki looked so pleased that I didn't say anything.

"I decided on a red collar. Like that red dress you like so much, Mizuho."

"My dress . . ."

"Yep. After all, he's your pet as well as mine."

Unusually for her she smiled, which completely obliterated any thought of danger I'd had before. Yuki had given my favorite color to her precious pet! I was so thrilled that I blushed.

"How sweet of you, Yuki, thanks. It's a cute collar, isn't it? It suits him."

I cautiously went up to Poochie and stroked his head. Poochie gave off the stench of a wild animal, and the pale skin on the top of his head felt sticky.

Poochie had just finished eating the bread rolls I'd given him when there was a knock on the door of the shed.

"Mizuho, are you there?"

Yuki came in, still wearing her school backpack. She'd obviously come here straight from finishing the class chores. "Poochie, come! I've brought you some milk, too," she said, taking a bottle of milk out of her backpack.

Poochie stared in delight, though slightly hesitantly, at the milk she held out to him.

"What's up, Poochie? It's for you. You can drink it!"

She poured some into his dish, and he started happily lapping it up.

"You're eating a lot today, aren't you, Poochie?" she said, stroking his head.

"He's already eaten three bread rolls, you know."

"He has? Poochie, you must have been hungry!"

I was in two minds about stroking Poochie's head. He was cute in a way, but touching him felt a bit creepy. But Yuki seemed totally okay with stroking his head and his stubble.

Yuki and I met up an hour before school every day and headed to the mountain together.

Poochie wasn't locked up at all, but he never ran away. He was always waiting obediently for us on all fours, and he never used his hands except to eat. Somehow I found that reassuring.

Yuki and I always held hands as we opened the door to the shed. On all fours, Poochie would look up at us with watery eyes.

He hardly ever made a sound. Just occasionally he would cry, "Finishitbytwo!" This was probably an order he used to issue before he became our pet.

I'd once asked Yuki where she'd found him. "Otema-chi," she said, referring to the business district near Tokyo

Station. "I had a test for cram school and had gone there on my own. And I saw Poochie wandering around, lost. So I took him home with me and fed him, and he got very attached to me. Then I thought of you, Mizuho. I thought it'd be cute to look after him together."

There was probably someone in Otemachi who was still looking for him. But even if his owner ever came to try to find him, Yuki and I were resolved to keeping him secret. Anyway, Poochie was really attached to us. He must like his life on the mountain behind our school better than his life in Otemachi.

One day we went to feed Poochie and found the door to the shed wide-open.

"Poochie?" Yuki called, running into the shed.

There were footprints from large shoes on the floor. Poochie was nowhere to be seen.

"Poochie? Poochie!"

"These footprints must be from Otemachi," I said, peering at them cautiously.

"Oh, no!" Yuki said, going pale. "Maybe he's gone back there?"

Yuki looked dejected, so I held out my arms to hug her, but just then there was a sound outside.

"Poochie!" Yuki cried, evading my clasp and running outside.

Crouching there was Poochie, his head and suit covered in leaves.

"Poochie, you're back! You're back!"

Yuki hugged him, stroking his head and back. He must have escaped his pursuer from Otemachi.

"Finishitbytwo!" Poochie cried quietly, closing his eyes in Yuki's arms.

Life Ceremony

I was having lunch in the meeting room with five women colleagues from the same department when one of them suddenly stopped eating and looked up, dangling her chopsticks in midair.

"Oh, I almost forgot. I heard that Mr. Nakao from General Affairs passed away."

We all looked at her.

"What? Really?"

"Seems it was a stroke."

I pictured Mr. Nakao's good-natured smile. He was an elegant man with silver-gray hair and often shared sweets he received from clients with us. He'd retired just a few years ago.

"So young!"

"You can say that again. When did it happen?"

"The day before yesterday, apparently. This morning the company was informed that the ceremony will be held tonight. They said the deceased would have wanted as many of us as possible to come along."

"Really? I'd better hold back on lunch today, then. Maybe I'll skip dessert."

We all put our custard desserts back, unopened, into the bag from the convenience store.

"I bet Mr. Nakao tastes good," said a woman a year older than me as she ate her pork and potato stew.

"Maybe a bit tough, don't you think? He was thin and muscular, after all."

"I've eaten someone with a similar physique as Mr. Nakao before, and he was actually quite tasty. A bit stringy, maybe, but smooth on the tongue."

"Really? They say you get better soup stock from men, don't they?"

"You'll be going, won't you, Ms. Iketani?" another woman asked me as she put away the bag of desserts. "To the life ceremony, that is."

"Ah, um . . . I'm not sure," I said vaguely, tilting my head doubtfully as I tucked into the noriben lunch box I'd bought at a nearby convenience store.

"Seriously? But why? Oh, come to think of it, you're one of those people who doesn't really eat human flesh, aren't you?"

"No, no—it's not that! I just have a bit of an upset stomach, and I'm on my period."

"Oh, on your period. No wonder." She nodded, apparently satisfied. "But you can get pregnant even on your period, you know. You really should go. It's a life ceremony! You might get inseminated, mightn't you?"

Laughing it off, I washed down the fried fish and excess sauce with some tea from a plastic bottle.

When I was little, it was forbidden to eat human flesh. I'm certain it was.

Now, however, the custom of eating flesh has become so deeply ingrained in our society that little by little, I'm becoming less confident about what things were like before. But thirty years ago, when I was still in kindergarten, I'm sure it was strictly taboo.

Riding the school bus, we'd already gotten tired of playing at word chains and had started naming things we wanted to eat. The children followed one after another, saying things like "A cloud! So soft and yummy!" "Candy floss! 'Cos it's sweet!" and then someone said, "An elephant! They're huge, and I'll feel stuffed after eating it!"

After that greedy child, others followed with the names of animals. "Well then, a giraffe!" "A monkey!" This last comment was from my best friend, and as a joke, I'd followed it unthinkingly with "A human!"

The whole bus erupted at my answer.

"Whaaat?"

"Creepy!"

Even my best friend was in tears. "Maho, I can't believe you'd say something so scary!!!" she stuttered, sobs punctuating her words and snot running from her nose.

In no time at all, like a chain reaction, everyone on the bus was crying and wailing.

After hearing what had happened, the teacher was furious with me. "Maho, you mustn't say things like that, even as a joke. You'll get into big trouble," she said, her face grim. I was crestfallen. I simply couldn't understand why it was okay to joke about eating a monkey, but not about eating a human.

Even now, I could still clearly recall the eyes of the stern-faced bus driver glaring at me, not to mention the terrifying expression on the face of our normally kind teacher and all my friends wailing behind her. I was scared stiff, sitting in the bus with my head bowed, unable to utter a single word.

All the humans on the bus, filled with righteousness, were reviling me. White-faced and tense, I shrank into my seat and held my breath. If anyone had shouted at me, my fear would have exploded and I would have wet myself.

Since then, however, the human race had changed little by little. The population shrank abruptly, and the world has become gripped with the fear that the human race might actually go extinct. This has had the effect of procreation morphing into a form of social justice.

We humans had gradually transformed over the past thirty years. Nowadays, few people ever talked about sex, referring to it rather as insemination with the specific aim of creating new life, and this became the mainstream view.

And whenever somebody died, it was customary to hold a type of ritual called a life ceremony instead of a funeral. Some people still held an old-fashioned wake and funeral, but financial subsidies were available for life ceremonies, so the vast majority opted for this considerably cheaper alternative.

Guests at a life ceremony would eat the deceased's body, and also seek an insemination partner among the other guests. As soon as a man and woman coupled off, they would leave the ceremony and go outside for insemination. Based on the idea of birthing life from death, this ceremony was a perfect fit for the mentality of the masses and their unconscious obsession with breeding.

Recently I'd been getting the feeling that humans had begun to resemble cockroaches in their habits. Cockroaches would apparently all gather to eat a deceased one of their number, and I'd also heard that a cockroach about to die would lay a huge number of eggs. Tribes that gathered to mourn and eat the deceased had existed since antiquity, though, so it wasn't as though the custom had only now just sprung up among humans.

Yamamoto lit up a 1mg American Spirit, then chuckled. "Are you telling me you still hold a grudge about something that happened to you as a kid?"

The smoking room at work was in one corner of a space we called the common room that had a vending machine and a few chairs. It was partitioned off by glass, and I often met people from other departments in there. It was here that I first got talking to Yamamoto, too.

Yamamoto was short and plump and good-natured, and, at thirty-nine, three years older than me. He was good-natured and I liked the way he always listened to what I had to say, and though he often laughed, he never laughed my opinions off. I always felt comfortable with him and ended up telling him things I wouldn't tell anyone else.

Sulkily I chewed the filter of my Hi-lite menthol cigarette. "It's not that I hold a grudge particularly. It's just that thirty years ago a completely different sense of values was the norm, and I just can't keep up with the changes. I kind of feel like I've been betrayed by the world."

Yamamoto blinked. His eyes were small and round, with long lashes. "Well, I guess I know what you mean. I think it was forbidden to eat human flesh around the time I was in kindergarten."

"Right? I'm totally certain it was! Yet nowadays everybody says it's such a great thing to do. That's what I can't get my head around."

"Oh well. So, what about tonight? Are you going to Mr. Nakao's life ceremony?"

"What about you?"

Yamamoto wasn't one of those who adamantly opposed eating human flesh, but he didn't particularly like to, so I found it reassuring when he was around. Even now that eating human flesh had become mainstream, there was still a deeply rooted faction opposed to it and groups campaigned against it, saying it was unethical. However, it wasn't that Yamamoto or I opposed eating it on ethical grounds. In Yamamoto's case, at the age of twelve he'd suffered a bout of food poisoning after eating some slightly raw flesh at his grandfather's life ceremony. In my case, I didn't think there was anything particularly wrong about eating human flesh—after all, when I was little I'd said that I wanted to eat it, even if it was a joke—but I felt indignant that the ethic by which I'd been judged had turned out not to exist in the first place.

"Maybe I'll go," Yamamoto said, scratching the back of his neck. "It'd be good if I end up inseminating someone."

"Really? Maybe I'll go too, then."

I'd run out of cigarettes, so I took one from Yamamoto's box of American Spirits. "Do you like these?" I asked him. "You only smoke more when they're weak, which means you spend more and it ends up being worse for your health, too."

"It's okay—I like them better like this." He blew out smoke, savoring the taste.

Not many people smoked, so Yamamoto and I had the space to ourselves.

It was tiny, less than one tatami mat in size, and looking out through the glass gave the sensation of being a goldfish in a bowl.

I blew out smoke from the cigarette I'd cadged from him. We chatted in the white fog we'd created from the smoke, gazing at the clear world outside.

That evening, Yamamoto and I headed out together to Mr. Nakao's life ceremony. The objective of a life ceremony was to give birth to new life, so skimpy clothing or showy outfits were the norm. I was still dressed in my gray work suit, but Yamamoto was wearing a red-checkered shirt with white pants.

"It's best to dress flashily for a life ceremony," he said cheerfully, but the outfit didn't really suit his dark complexion.

Mr. Nakao's house was in an expensive residential area in Setagaya ward. It was dinnertime, and cooking smells hung in the air all around. No doubt Mr. Nakao's flesh being boiled was mixed in with them.

"Here it is," said Yamamoto, checking the map on his phone. It was a large house, beginning to show signs of age, and an aroma of miso came from inside.

"Miso soup! Maybe with some white miso mixed in? Smells delicious!" Yamamoto said happily, sniffing the air as he went inside.

In the entrance hall, a sign on pink paper read MASARU NAKAO LIFE CEREMONY.

We called out "Good evening" as we opened the door, and an elegant white-haired woman wearing an apron, apparently Mrs. Nakao, came out to greet us.

"Oh, so good of you to come. Please do come in. We're just about to start," she said, ushering us through to the living room. Two large earthenware cooking pots were already on the table in the center of the room, which had been decorated with lots of seasonal flowers. It occurred to me that the pots must have been the beloved possessions of Mr. Nakao when he was alive. For many years, he had used them for cooking rice with seasonal ingredients, which he would share with us at work.

Human flesh has quite a strong smell and taste, so it isn't considered suitable for simple grilling with a little salt and pepper. Most people thoroughly parboil it, then add it to a hotpot with vegetables and plenty of miso for flavor. And it is common to have a specialist company help with the preparation. As I went in, a number of men in overalls were on their way out, bowing their heads as they left.

Men and women dressed to the nines were seated around the hotpots. Some of them were already exchanging flirtatious looks and starting a conversation with someone they found attractive. It appeared the life ceremony was already well underway.

"Thank you, everyone, for coming to my husband's life ceremony," Mrs. Nakao said, opening the lids of the hotpots to reveal Mr. Nakao, boiled together with Chinese cabbage, enoki mushrooms, and other vegetables. "Please partake of his life, and create new life."

"*Itadakimasu!*"

Everybody held their hands together and gave thanks for the meal, then began tucking into Mr. Nakao, praising him as they took neat, thin slices of his meat to their mouths.

"Delicious! Mrs. Nakao, your husband is really tasty."

A white-haired elderly man nodded as he put some meat into his mouth. "It really is a good custom, isn't it? We partake of life, we create life . . ."

Mrs. Nakao dabbed her eyes with a handkerchief upon hearing these words. "That's right. My husband will be pleased, too," she said. "These parts over here are the ones closest to the innards, and really tasty. Please do eat them up. You youngsters, eat as much life as you can, then get on with insemination."

The elderly man tried to give me a bowl of the meat, so I hastily said, "Just some Chinese cabbage for me."

"I'll have some shiitake and enoki mushrooms," said Yamamoto.

"Oh? You two dislike human flesh, do you?" the old man said, tilting his head in bemusement.

"It's not that, it's just I got food poisoning from it once long ago," Yamamoto replied. "Ever since, I always seem to get diarrhea whenever I try it, so I prefer to stick to vegetables, really."

"And having heard this, I also find it hard to eat it . . . I'm sorry," I apologized. It was a lot of work to prepare a human body for cooking. Even with the help of professionals, Mrs. Nakao must have been hard at work since morning.

She smiled sadly and served me some Chinese cabbage. "It's okay, don't worry. But Mr. Nakao would be so pleased if you ate him, so please do help yourself anytime you feel like it."

Just then a young woman in a pink dress and a man in a white jacket stood up, holding hands. They had been whispering to each other and touching knees as they ate the flesh hotpot.

"Well, we're going to go ahead with insemination now."

"Oh, I'm so glad to hear that. Congratulations!"

There was some applause as the couple bowed to Mrs. Nakao. "Thank you so much. We will do our best to create a new life," they said, and left, still holding hands.

"Wouldn't it be wonderful if Mr. Nakao were reborn in a new life!" Yamamoto said with a smile. He drank some of the soup made with the stock from Mr. Nakao's body.

"Wouldn't it!" Mrs. Nakao said. "I wonder how many inseminations will happen tonight? I do hope lots of new lives will be created!" She gazed affectionately at the pots. The soup made from red and white miso mixed together was a rich brown color, and you couldn't really see Mr. Nakao inside it.

In the end, Yamamoto and I took our leave from the life ceremony, neither of us having found an insemination partner.

Yamamoto slipped and almost fell as we walked along a back alley. "Argh!"

"Are you okay? Have you had too much to drink?"

"No, it's not that."

Yamamoto looked sadly at his shoe. He'd apparently stepped in some semen that had spilled on the street.

I'd heard that in the old days, sex was considered dirty, and it was normal to do it out of sight. I'd never been inseminated at a life ceremony, but it was true that whenever I'd done it with a lover, we'd always used a bedroom or some other place where we wouldn't be seen. The old customs were probably still left in my body, even if I wasn't aware of them.

Nevertheless, insemination after a life ceremony was generally considered sacred and could be carried out anywhere. I'd seen it being done on the street at night any number of times, and it looked to me just like plain copulation. I had the feeling that humans were becoming more and more like animals.

"So they've built another center out here too, eh?" Yamamoto said, his breath smelling of alcohol.

He was referring to another children's center. Of course, children conceived during insemination were mostly raised in a family, but recently there were more and more cases where nobody knew who the child's father was. This was particularly true of pregnancies that followed life ceremonies. But the priority was to increase the population, so everyone was happy about the children born in these circumstances too.

As a result, centers were set up to take care of children so that women could carry on working while also producing children whenever they wanted to. After giving birth in the hospital within the center itself, some mothers simply left the baby there while others took the baby home for a while and delivered it to the center later. Roughly half of the children were raised in a family, and half were left as babies for the center to raise.

Many people were strongly against the centers, as they believed it would lead to the family system breaking down. The new childbirth system evidently hadn't received the same level of acceptance as life ceremonies. Nevertheless, at this rate, more and more children were likely to be raised outside the family system, and it was no longer possible to predict what would become of the human race. Various researchers were publishing their findings, expressing both positive and pessimistic views.

We may be headed in a dangerous direction, but the vague conclusion seemed to be that we wouldn't know unless we tried.

"I wonder what will happen if more and more children are raised at centers," Yamamoto murmured.

Nobody knew the answer to that. All I knew was that we were undergoing radical changes in society.

"Good morning!"

A woman who had been off work the last two weeks was greeted back in the office with a round of applause. At the age of thirty-six, she had taken leave to give birth to her third child.

"Did you pop the baby out at the center?"

"Yep, and I'm leaving it to them. I'm exhausted!"

"Thank you."

"Good job, well done."

Everyone was grateful for her having given birth for the benefit of the human race. She looked pleased as she accepted the bouquet of flowers presented to her.

At the centers, children were carefully raised as children of the human race, not of individual parents. The facilities were well equipped, and there was one counselor for every five children.

I had been inseminated by a lover, but it hadn't resulted in pregnancy, and I was relieved to see women like her who had given birth to lots of children. I was a member of the human race too, so I suppose I was keen for my own animal species to continue.

After accepting the bouquet, the woman went to her desk.

"I've been inseminated by my lover many times, but all three pregnancies were from a life ceremony," she said. "It's amazing, isn't it? It seems the pregnancy rate from life ceremonies is pretty high."

"Miraculous!" a younger woman said, enraptured.

"I can see why, really. Human meat is special, isn't it? It feels sacred, and it tastes good too."

"I hear you. I feel like it's human instinct to want to eat human flesh."

I felt like pointing out that until a moment ago they had been talking about a different human instinct. Instinct doesn't exist. Morals don't exist. They were just fake sensibilities that came from a world that was constantly transforming.

"What's up, Maho? You look angry!"

"No, not at all," I said quietly, and drank up the rest of my tea.

"Don't you think everyone's being weird with this instinct thing?" I asked Yamamoto. I drained my glass of beer in one gulp, slammed it down on the counter, and glared at him.

It was only Monday, but I really felt like having a drink and, having bumped into him in the smoking room, I'd dragged him out with me to an izakaya near the office.

He was the only person I could talk to about these kinds of things.

Yamamoto listened to me, nodding now and then, without agreeing or disagreeing. It was that sense of respect for distance that made me feel comfortable with him.

"You know," I said, "when it comes to insemination, my mother said that back in the old days, it was good manners to wear a condom when you had sex. Do that now, and you're told off for copulating for pleasure and not in order to give birth to new life. It doesn't make any sense!"

"Well, there's no need to get so worked up about it," Yamamoto said, leisurely taking a piece of fried chicken to his mouth.

"Listen to me!"

"I am. But you know, you're a bit stubborn. You're the one who sees things in absolutes. It's like you want to have everything your way."

"What do you mean?"

Yamamoto put down his chopsticks, wiped his hands with the disposable towel, and pursed his lips, his expression unusually stern.

"Seriously, though," he said. "It's the way the world is, right? Everyone always says that things like common sense or instinct or morals are carved in stone. But that's not true—actually, they're always changing. That's what I think. And this isn't something that's happened all of a sudden, like you seem to think. It's always been that way. Things keep transforming."

"If that's the case, I wish they'd stop judging people! It's like their position has been the right one for the last hundred million years or something. If it's always changing, it means it's not certain, right? And even though it's uncertain, everyone believes in it like a religion. It's so weird."

He shrugged. "Well, anyway, the world is but a brilliant mirage, a temporary illusion. I mean, it's an illusion you can only see now, so how about enjoying it to the full while you can?" He picked up his chopsticks again and started putting some pork kimchi and chorizo on his plate.

"Have some veggies too," I commented. "It's not good for you to eat only meat."

"No way. Omnivorous animals aren't supposed to taste very good, are they? When I ate human flesh as a kid, I thought it tasted great, but that's because Grandpa was a vegetarian. So I've decided to be a meat-arian in order to be tasty when it's my turn."

"Oh, c'mon!"

"Anyway. Eat delicious food, enjoy life, and taste good when I die so that those who eat me can summon the energy to give birth to new life. I don't think that's such a bad life. Oh, thanks."

He took the freshly heated flask of sake with a smile, poured himself some, and began drinking.

Feeling irritable, I was about to light a cigarette when Yamamoto chuckled and glanced around the lively izakaya.

"You know what? I don't think this world is all that bad. And I don't think the world that you remember from thirty years ago was bad either. It's always changed over time. The world here and now is just a momentary tint."

"Huh?"

"I really like Disneyland, you know."

"Ugh." I screwed up my face. "I hate it."

"I thought so." He chuckled. As always when he laughed, his small round eyes went all black and his long eyelashes fluttered. "Nobody ever mentions the person inside the cartoon-character costume, do they? Everyone's lying a bit. That's what makes it a dream country. Our world isn't any different, is it? Everyone keeps telling little lies, and that's how the mirage is created. That's why it's beautiful—because it's a momentary make-believe world."

"What about the real world? Where the hell is that, then?"

"It's the mirage that's real. All our little lies are gathered together and become a reality that you can see only now."

"I don't understand. I don't want to understand!"

Yamamoto laughed, and some sake spilled out of his cup. "Life must be tough for you, Iketani! Why not just enjoy yourself in this momentary world of lies?"

I blew out smoke. Maybe he was right. Maybe the world hadn't just started transforming recently and we had been continually changing long before thirty years ago.

Even though I could understand the logic of what Yamamoto was saying, I was probably hoping for some kind of concrete certainty. That felt terribly childish. I felt a chill around my shoulders and rubbed them to warm up, then drank down my shochu topped up with hot water.

Yamamoto patted me on the back. "Don't overthink things!" he teased. "When you go to an amusement park, you don't wonder how the roller coaster is put together or how a merry-go-round is powered, do you? Just relax and live your life!"

I felt warmed by the comforting feeling of his hand rhythmically patting my spine and the taste of the strong alcohol flowing down my throat.

Yamamoto had something of a teddy bear about him. When I told him this, he said sadly, "Yes, there is. And that's why women never fancy me."

I burst out laughing. All of a sudden the chill had left me, and Yamamoto removed his large, warm hand from my back and took out a cigarette. The white smoke rising from where he was sitting on my right clouded my vision. Through the fog, Yamamoto's long eyelashes fluttered as he laughed.

* * *

That weekend, I heard that Yamamoto was dead.

I was in my apartment doing the laundry. It was the first time in ages we'd had nice weather on the weekend, and I had just put some pillowcases and cushion covers into the washing machine when the phone rang. It was a colleague, a younger woman.

Yamamoto had apparently been on his way home on Friday night, after being out drinking with a friend from college days, when he was hit by a car. He didn't have much in the way of visible injuries, but he'd hit his head badly.

"His life ceremony is tonight. You'll go, won't you, Iketani? You got along well with him, after all . . ." I could hear her sniveling as she spoke.

I don't remember how I answered, or even when I hung up. The next thing I knew, I was kneeling on the floor, gripping my cell phone. I badly wanted to call Yamamoto and ask him if it was true that he had died.

I don't know how long I remained sitting there in a daze. I heard the washing machine beep for the end of the cycle, and I stood up reflexively. Moving mechanically, I mutely hung the pillowcases and cushion covers up to dry. I knew it wasn't the time to be doing this, but I didn't know what else to do.

My parents were still going strong, and my grandparents had died before I was born, so it was my first experience of someone close to me dying. The movement of my hands and the sensation of the wet cushion cover felt distant. As I came back inside from the balcony, I staggered and caught hold of the mosquito screen.

Just then my phone rang again.

"Hello. Is this Maho Iketani?"

"Um, yes?"

"I'm Keisuke Yamamoto's mother." I held my breath, and the voice continued. "I'm sorry to call you suddenly like this. It's just that your name comes up a lot in my son's phone call history . . ."

"Oh . . . I mean, I knew him from work. He was very kind to me. He, um . . . please accept my deepest sympathies for your loss," I stuttered.

"Oh, I *am* sorry! So you were his work colleague . . . I thought you might be a close friend."

It appeared that she'd mistaken me for her son's girl-friend or something. Come to think of it, Yamamoto had complained that although his mother wasn't opposed to life ceremonies, she was against the breakdown of the family system and was always going on at him to start a proper family rather than having a child brought up in a center. To stop her from worrying, he'd even told her that he had a steady girlfriend and didn't really bother with life cer-emony inseminations. In reality, however, there was no such person in his life, and since mine was the female name that occurred most often in his call history, she had assumed it must be me.

"Um, Yamamoto was in a different department, but he was a good friend, and we often used to go out drinking together. I would like to come to today's life ceremony too, if I may."

"Thank you. My son would be delighted."

"What time will it start?"

I must have heard this from the earlier call, but I had no recollection of it at all and felt again how very shaken up I was. I needed to hold on to something, and realized I was already gripping my skirt with my free hand.

"Well, we're planning to start around six p.m., but it might have to be a bit later . . ."

"Oh, really?"

"My daughter and I are busy with the preparations, but we're not making very good progress, so I think it'll probably be a bit later."

"Are you arranging it just between the two of you?" I was surprised. It was a huge amount of work to prepare for a life ceremony, so people usually got the professionals in, unless there were very good reasons not to. They couldn't possibly do the whole thing by themselves, I thought. "Er, would you like me to come and help?"

"What?"

"Yamamoto was a friend, so . . . please do let me help," I insisted, given her hesitation.

After I got her to agree, I immediately started getting ready to leave. I changed into some old jeans and trainers that I didn't mind getting dirty and immediately went over to Yamamoto's place.

It was imperative to serve human meat fresh, so unless there was any sign of foul play, the body was usually taken to the professionals right away. The accident had happened the night before last, so Yamamoto's meat must be ready for cooking by now.

Yamamoto's condo was in central Tokyo. When I arrived, his mother opened the auto-lock to let me in the building and hastily came out to greet me.

"I'm so sorry about this," she said.

"No, really, it's fine. I'm not sure how much use I'll be, but . . ."

The polystyrene boxes containing Yamamoto had just been delivered and were still sitting in the hall.

"We don't have many relatives, so the two of us are basically his only immediate family . . . I should have asked the professionals to do the cooking for us too, but it was a bit difficult for various reasons, and we decided to do it ourselves . . ."

"What do you mean, difficult?"

Yamamoto's mother smiled uncomfortably. "He left detailed recipes. If you get the professionals to do it, all you'll get is miso hotpot. My son apparently didn't like that, and wants us to make him into meatballs in a grated daikon hotpot."

"Grated daikon hotpot . . . ?"

I was taken aback. Human meat was known for having a gamy taste, so it was standard to use strong flavorings with it. Would it be okay to use it in a hotpot that was known for its delicate flavor? My unease must have shown, as his mother nodded.

"It's not going to be easy, but . . . I mean, that boy was such a foodie. He always was fussy about food, and it's no different with the meal we are to make with his flesh. It isn't just hotpot, you know. Stir-fry with cashew nuts, braised meat . . ."

"What? Not just hotpot?"

"That's right. I want to respect his will as much as possible, but really, it's a tall order!"

"Can I see the recipes?"

I looked at the file she held out for me. It contained numerous recipes on loose-leaf paper, organized according to ingredients. It was just like Yamamoto, a keen cook who loved food, to do something like this, I thought. There were numerous headings, such as pork, chicken, salmon, cabbage, daikon, and so forth, and at the very end was a final category: "My flesh."

I leafed through that section to see that it was just as his mother had said, with detailed recipes for "Cashew Nut and Me Stir-Fry," "Meatballs of Me in Grated Daikon Hotpot," and so forth.

"It looks like he just jotted them down when they occurred to him," his mother said, "and didn't necessarily mean it as a will to follow. But still, he did write them down, and somehow it makes me want to respect his dying wishes . . ."

"I understand."

It was true. Yamamoto had always gone on about wanting everyone to have a wonderful time at his own life ceremony.

He had jotted down instructions in tiny letters in the corners of the recipes, things like "Decorate the room cheerfully, like at Christmas"; "I really want everyone to savor this one"; "Make it a splendid ceremony so that there will be lots of insemination!"

Yamamoto had always had this girly side to him. The words in the recipes began to blur, and I hastily closed the file and rolled up my sleeves.

"Anyway, let's get on with it. Where's the arm flesh?"

"In a box out there."

I was just getting on with things in the kitchen when I heard the door open, and Yamamoto's younger sister came in.

"I'm back! I bought some mizuna and daikon and—oh! Hello!" she said, apparently surprised to see me.

"I—er—I've come over to help," I said, bowing my head in greeting.

"She's from Keisuke's workplace," the mother explained simply.

The daughter frowned. "You see? I told you he didn't have a girlfriend. He was too vain . . . I'm sorry that you got roped in like this."

"No, not at all. Yamamoto was really kind to me."

I couldn't very well say that he was a smoking partner, so I simply took the supermarket shopping bags from his sister. They were stuffed full of items from Yamamoto's recipes, like mizuna and cashew nuts.

"Okay, well, in that case, please do help. We'd better start with the more complex recipes or we'll never be ready in time." Glancing at the clock, she hurriedly tied her hair back.

I nodded. "Sure. I'll start making the meatballs."

I went out into the hall and looked at the Styrofoam boxes piled up there. There were seven or eight of them, filled with dry ice, so they felt cool to the touch.

All the difficult jobs, like draining his blood, skinning him, removing his innards, and processing waste and the part around his anus and so forth had been done by the professionals, and what was in the boxes was Yamamoto turned into meat on the bone. Normally the flesh was removed from the bone and sliced thinly, ready to put into the hotpot; this was the first time I'd ever seen human flesh prepared in various shapes and forms.

Yamamoto had been a bit worried about developing metabolic syndrome, but now, with him turned into meat, I could see that he wasn't as fatty as I'd expected.

Seeing the fresh red mixed with white, I thought how pretty he was.

I found the box with ARM MEAT written on it, lifted it up, and took it into the kitchen. I took out Yamamoto's arms, skinned and drained of blood, and began the task of cutting the flesh away from the bone. Meanwhile, his sister rushed in with another Styrofoam box and took out Yamamoto's thighs.

"Okay," she said. "I'll get on with preparing the meat for braising. Mom, can you boil some water to be ready for parboiling?"

With his sister briskly issuing instructions, we quickly got on with making Yamamoto into the recipes he'd prepared.

The professionals had done a good amount of the work for us, but you could still make out the form of Yamamoto in the meat. He and I had often gone out drinking together, and now, as I stripped the flesh from the bone, I remembered his strong, hairy arms lifting his beer glass.

These very arms had patted me on the back when I was down, and had dragged me out of the road when I was unsteady on my feet after drinking too much. Once, in the smoking room, I'd dropped ash on his arm, and he'd blown on the red patch and said reproachfully, "Ouch, that's hot."

And just last Monday this hand had given me an encouraging pat on the back. His big, gentle arms were now meat on the bone, lying quietly on the chopping board.

"It's the first time I've ever cooked human meat," I said. "It's chunky, isn't it? The only time I've seen raw human meat at a life ceremony, it had already been cut into thin slices."

"Oh, really? Yes, it is chunky. Not like chicken or something. You can use milk to get rid of the smell, you know. It might be a good idea to soak it awhile before braising it."

Stripping the meat off Yamamoto's arm bone was hard work, a bit like dealing with a giant chicken wing. When I was done, I put Yamamoto, now just bone, back into the Styrofoam box, then started grinding batches of his meat in the food processor. It was slow going, and we'd never make it in time with that alone, so his mother was also mincing some with a kitchen knife.

Together we put Yamamoto into bowls, added some starch, onions, sake, and so forth, and then kneaded him before making him into a heap of meatballs. Meanwhile, his sister grated several large daikon radishes.

His mother had put two large pots of water on to boil. After seasoning the water with grated ginger, soup stock, and sake, we checked the flavor, then started putting in the meatballs.

Lastly we added enoki mushrooms, grated daikon, and mizuna, followed by sliced green onions and Chinese cabbage.

There wasn't quite enough grated daikon, so I was grating some more when a pleasant aroma rose from the frying pan. Yamamoto's sister was making the cashew-nut stir-fry.

"You're a good cook, aren't you," I said.

"It's my hobby," she said shyly. "I go to cookery classes. Though it never occurred to me that they might come in handy for something like this, though."

Now that the meatballs were cooking, we started on the braised meat. The recipe indicated braising the meat in salt, which tended to bring out a strong flavor. I took out the chunks that his sister had marinated in milk. The meat from Yamamoto's thigh was bigger and heavier than I'd expected, and I thought that he probably had been suffering from metabolic syndrome after all.

I diced the meat and put it into a large pot, added green onions, garlic, and ginger, and brought it to a boil. Thanks to the milk, it didn't smell too strong, but it wasn't yet cooked enough for a bamboo skewer to pass through.

"Looks like it's going to take some time," I said.

"While it's cooking, shall we decorate the room?"

We covered the meat with aluminum foil and left it to simmer while we started tidying up Yamamoto's apartment. For seating, we placed his kotatsu in the center of the living room and alongside it two folding tables his mother had brought. It was quite a large apartment for someone living alone, but with three tables, there wasn't much space for people to sit.

"It'll be a bit cramped, but it can't be helped."

"People will be coming and going. It'll be fine."

Yamamoto's sister began decorating the room with flowers and wreaths, as indicated in the scribbles on his recipes.

Meanwhile, the braising meat was tender enough to add some broth, sake, salt, and black pepper and put it back on to simmer on a low heat for a bit longer. When it was more or less done, we seasoned it with watercress, yuzu-flavored pepper paste, Japanese pepper, and mustard. We'd just served it up on a large dish when the doorbell rang.

"Do come in!" his sister said into the interphone, opening the auto-lock door. It was time for the life ceremony to begin. Hurriedly, I added some yuzu peel to the reheated large hotpot for the finishing touch.

Yamamoto's condo was full of people who had come for his life ceremony.

"I'm sorry . . . we should have rented a larger venue," his mother said, opening some red wine and bringing it to the table.

"Miss Iketani, the hotpot should be ready now," his sister said to me as she attended to the frying pan, so I nodded at her and took the Yamamoto grated daikon hotpot into the living room.

"Oh! Daikon hotpot!"

"Wow!"

A chorus of exclamations went up, and everyone peered into the pot.

"There's ponzu sauce and yuzu, so please help yourself. And here's some more grated daikon too, so be sure to add it as you eat."

"Iketani, did you come to help out?" asked some of my colleagues who had come along.

"Yes, that's how it ended up. Please eat as much as you like!"

"Thank you!"

Just then, Yamamoto's sister came in with the cashew-nut stir-fry and the stew. "Sorry to have kept you waiting," she said.

"Oh my, so it's not just hotpot?"

"Amazing! That must have been so much work."

Seeing everyone's beaming faces, I felt somehow proud. Yamamoto was the sort of guy who liked to see everyone looking happy. It was perfectly fitting to his character to wish for such a warm atmosphere at his own life ceremony.

Just as he had hoped, everyone was smiling. I thought he must be the only person in the whole world to have been made into such a sumptuous feast.

After each of the various meat dishes had been met with applause as they were lined up on the table, Yamamoto's sister said, "Well then, let's begin."

Everyone put their hands together, said "*Itadakimasu*," then started eating.

"Come on, you too, Iketani!"

I sat down at the end of the table and helped myself to a plateful of Yamamoto meatballs.

"I thought you didn't like human meat, Iketani," a younger colleague said in surprise.

"Oh no, it's not that I don't like it. It's just that it usually gives me an upset stomach," I replied. "But today it's daikon hotpot, so I'll stuff myself!"

I picked up my chopsticks, placed an entire Yamamoto meatball steeped in broth in my mouth, and gently chewed.

The meat juices spread through my mouth, filling it with different flavors: the acidity of the yuzu juice, the fresh-mouth feel of the grated daikon, and the mellow yet full flavor of the meat, stronger than beef or pork but not as gamy as wild boar.

"Oof, it's hot!" I huffed with my mouth open, relishing the taste. It was not at all strong-tasting, as we had prepared it so thoroughly, nor was it gristly, despite being ground meat.

The umami of the meat blended with the tang of the broth and slowly melted on my tongue. The slightly spicy grated daikon covering the meatballs added an extra accent, enhancing the flavor.

Next I served myself some of the Yamamoto braised meat. It was packed with flavor. The yuzu pepper paste really suited the rich flavor of human meat. The condiments had elegantly settled the slight tang of wild animal, and it would have gone well with some white rice. The more I chewed on it, the mix of firm and chewy chunks of meat with the plump, fatty bits yielded an even deeper flavor. I added a little mustard, which drew out yet more umami, and the meat and its juices spread through my mouth.

"I always thought red wine was best suited for human meat, but this would go well with white too, wouldn't it?"

"There's some white too, if you like," Yamamoto's mother said as she went around happily filling people's glasses.

The life ceremony that day was a grand celebration. A lot of people came and went, and many couples paired off for insemination and left hand in hand.

The hotpot was emptied any number of times, and we kept bringing in more vegetables and meatballs from the kitchen to replenish it.

People who had loved Yamamoto were eating him, using his life force to create new life.

For the first time, it occurred to me that the life ceremony was actually a wonderful ritual. I was completely absorbed in eating Yamamoto, and also running around bringing in more of him to replenish the dishes.

The dreamlike event came to an end, the meatballs and braised meat were finished, and the life ceremony was declared over.

As we were clearing up afterward, Yamamoto's sister came over to me with two Tupperware boxes.

"Miss Iketani, thank you so much for all your help today. Please take this home with you."

Inside was some of the Yamamoto cashew stir-fry and some rice balls.

"Oh, are you sure?"

"I put some aside for you before it was all eaten up. I didn't have any special ingredients for the rice balls, so I just filled them with some of the braised meat. You were so busy that you didn't really get to eat much. Please have it as a late-night snack, or something. It's not much, but a small token of our gratitude."

"That's lovely. Thank you so much," I said, taking the Tupperware boxes of food. It had gone cold, but the delicious aroma still rose from it.

I left Yamamoto's condo and suddenly decided to go and have a picnic. I had some rice balls and a dish to go with them. Apart from anything, I was too worked up to sleep even if I did go straight home.

I saw traces of semen here and there in the area around Yamamoto's condo. Hopefully it was all from people who had paired off for insemination at the ceremony. I had the feeling that Yamamoto's life, like the fluff from a dandelion, had flown out into the world.

The late train I'd taken finally came out by the seaside in Kamakura.

Yamamoto had loved the sea. When we'd gone on the company trip to Misaki Port, he'd rolled up his jeans to go paddling in the water, ignoring everyone who tried to stop him, and his clothes had gotten soaked.

The seaside is great. Humans have lived by the ocean since ancient times, so our DNA responds to it fondly. That's what he'd said at the time.

This was the world that Yamamoto had treasured. We humans were here for only a moment, the time it takes to blink in the flow of time experienced by the big lump we call Earth. In that enormously long moment, we continued to evolve and transform. I was here in a momentary scene of the never-ending kaleidoscope.

I slowly opened the Tupperware boxes. Three rice balls filled with Yamamoto braised meat were neatly packed inside one, and in the other was some of the Yamamoto cashew stir-fry, with lots of red peppers and other vegetables.

"Um, what are you doing?" a voice suddenly asked.

I turned around in surprise. A man I didn't know was standing there with a flashlight.

"Oh, I'm sorry."

"No, not at all . . . I live in the neighborhood and happened to see you walking unsteadily toward the sea at night, and I was a little worried about you."

He must have thought I was about to commit suicide. I held up the boxes of food for him to see.

"I'm just having a picnic. I'm sorry to have surprised you."

"No, no, it's fine . . . but it's a weird time of night to be having a picnic, isn't it?"

"This is a friend of mine called Yamamoto. I've been at his life ceremony all day, and I was given these leftovers, so brought them here to eat."

"Oh, I see."

"Um, would you like to share him with me?" I asked, thinking it'd be quite nice to have someone to talk to, but the man tilted his head to one side, uncertain of how to respond.

"I'd like to, but since you're talking about a life ceremony . . . I mean, I'm gay."

I held out a rice ball for him. "It's okay. I didn't mean it like that. The food is made from recipes my friend himself devised."

The man peered curiously into the boxes and sat down next to me.

"That is unusual, isn't it? I've only ever eaten human meat in a miso hotpot."

"That's the usual way. But it's also delicious stir-fried like this."

"Well, if you're sure you don't mind."

We started eating the food, watching the nighttime sea.

"This is delicious. Actually, I hadn't had dinner yet and was feeling hungry."

"I'm so glad. Please eat as much as you like."

Fragments of Yamamoto were being scattered out into the world, turning into energy in people's stomachs. That delighted me enormously.

"Having eaten this, it's a pity I can't carry out the insemination, isn't it? If it wasn't so late, I'm sure there would have been a lovely man for you to do it with around here."

"No worries. It's not like I absolutely have to do it." I smiled and then burst out laughing. "Put like that, it kind of makes us sound like plants sending out pollen, doesn't it? When a life ends, it flies far away and fertilizes new life."

"True. Yeah, that's the way it is. Pretty mysterious when you think about it."

"But then, if I'm a pistil, it would be odd for me to fly."

"Why? So what if a pistil flies?" The man picked up some of the cashew stir-fry with his disposable chopsticks and carried it to his mouth.

"Yamamoto's cashew-nut stir-fry really is super delicious," he added, narrowing his eyes in pleasure.

"Right? He goes well with cashew nuts, doesn't he? I never realized it when he was still alive."

I listened to the sound of the ocean, then suddenly thought of something.

"Um, can you remember what it was like thirty years ago?"

"What?"

I bit into a rice ball, feeling somehow like I was floating in the sound of the waves. Maybe I was still a little drunk from the wine.

"Back then we didn't have the custom of eating human meat," I murmured. "Do you remember that time?"

"Oh . . . but I wasn't born yet. I've only just turned twenty-four. When I was little, it was already kind of normal to eat it."

"Oh, I see . . ."

The man tilted his head inquiringly as if to ask, What about it?

"What if people back then could see us eating Yamamoto in a cashew-nut stir-fry now?" I blurted out. "They'd think we were out of our minds, wouldn't they?"

He thought about it for a moment, then nodded. "Yes, I think they would."

"Do you think that's strange? The world is changing so fast I no longer know what's right or wrong, and now we are here following the current custom eating Yamamoto like this. Do you think we're weird?"

He shook his head. "No, I don't. I mean, normal is a type of madness, isn't it? I think it's just that the only madness society allows is called normal."

"Eh?"

"So I think it's fine. As things are now, Yamamoto is delicious and we are normal to think so, even if people in a hundred years' time think we're mad."

I listened to the sound of the waves. The sound Yamamoto had loved.

The man finished eating his rice ball and stood up. "Thank you so much for sharing that. I'd better be going now."

"Okay."

"Are you sure you don't want me to accompany you back into town?"

"No, that's fine. I want to walk a little more; then I'll find somewhere to stay for the night."

"Okay, then."

We said goodbye, and I walked along the beach.

There was a couple engaged in insemination on the beach. What would that have looked like back when it was still called sex? Was it treated as a sacred action the way insemination is now? Or was it considered dirty? It must have been considered dirty, given that it was done out of sight.

I was vaguely wondering about such things when I felt a tap on my back.

Surprised, I turned to see the man again.

"Sorry to make you jump. Um . . . this is for you."

"What?"

He held out a small bottle. "I put it in there just now, so please do accept it."

I peered at the bottle and saw a white liquid inside it.

"I went to the toilets to do it. They say it dies when it comes into contact with the air, so I don't know whether it'll work. But I wanted to do what I could for Yamamoto's life ceremony."

"Thank you!"

I took the still-warm bottle from him. "I'm so happy. I'm sure it's still alive. I heard somewhere that sperm is protected by the outer layer of semen, so even when it comes into contact with the air, it can live for three days in the right conditions. Thank you so much! I'll use it very carefully."

He was sweating slightly from his recent effort. "You're welcome. Yamamoto really was delicious. I hardly ever go to life ceremonies, but having eaten him, I wanted to participate even if only in some small way," he said with a smile.

"I'm so pleased. Yamamoto would be happy too." I looked at the bottle in my hand.

"The bottle originally had star sand in it. It was in my bag, and the only suitable container I had at hand."

"Are you sure, really? It's so pretty," I murmured. The white liquid teeming with life was so pretty that I wanted to think it was the star sand itself.

"Wow, what's going on?" the man muttered suddenly, as if surprised.

"What?"

"Incredible! Did you bring them with you?"

I turned and saw that all of a sudden there were a lot of people on the beach. I strained my eyes for a closer look and realized that they were all engaged in insemination.

"Whenever there's a life ceremony, the beaches around here are always full of people doing this. I didn't hear of anything happening today, though." He tilted his head, puzzled. "Well, there wasn't any need for me to bring that bottle after all, was there?" He sounded quite embarrassed.

"Oh no, not at all. I'll use it! Definitely, I'll inseminate myself with it."

He laughed bashfully. "Okay, I'll be off now, then," he said, and left.

Now that I was on my own, I rolled my jeans up to the knees and walked into the sea.

The beach was full of people engaged in insemination, their white arms dimly flickering as they writhed on the sand.

It was like a scene from antiquity, ancient life-forms coming out of the sea onto the land. I hadn't witnessed such a thing, but what was happening that night felt like a nostalgic, important memory, and I watched the white shapes and black waves unblinkingly. I could understand Yamamoto's fondness for the ocean.

I made my way between the copulating couples, the waves lapping at my legs as I moved deeper into the water.

The entangled bodies resembled plants in the moonlight. I carried on through the numerous white trees, a whole forest immersed in water.

I carried on until I was up to my knees in the water, then pulled my jeans down. I poured the white liquid from the bottle into my hand and slowly inserted it into my body.

Semen spilled from my fingertips.

Yamamoto's life, dispersed from the warm meal in his condo into the ocean and into the world.

Maybe a miracle would occur, and I would conceive. Even if I didn't, the world in which we exchanged sperm like this somehow struck me as beautiful.

As I stood there enveloped in the sound of the waves, semen trickled down my legs. Water teeming with life caressed my thighs.

Right now, in the absolute normality that existed only in this brief moment in the long flow of time on this planet, semen was being sucked up into my body.

For the first time in my life I dissolved into this normality. Dyed by the colors of the ever-changing world, I became part of the tint of this unique moment.

The night deepened, and the sky and sea turned pitch-black. Yamamoto's life was slowly absorbed into my flesh. As I blended with him into one life, I closed my eyes, my legs still immersed in our beloved water. The sound of the waves caressed the eardrums of all of us there engaged in insemination.

Body Magic

"How come you and Shiho Hashimoto are friends, Ruri?"

I was sitting chatting with Aki and Miho when they suddenly came out with this. "It's so weird. I mean, you're in the same club at school, but you're totally different types."

We were in our second year of junior high school, and some of the girls in our class were rounding out and beginning to look like adult women, while others still had boyish bodies, their contours hardly changed since elementary school.

I was often mistaken for being in senior high school, or even for a college student sometimes, maybe because of my almost waist-length straight black hair or the fact that I'd grown so tall. Or because, as everyone kept saying, I had big breasts. My friends were always saying I acted so grown up, too. Shiho, on the other hand, still looked young enough to slip on her elementary school backpack at any moment, and when we were together, we must have really stood out as incongruous.

Shiho hadn't grown at all since starting junior high. Her school uniform was still too big for her, and when she held her arms up, you could see the white skin under her armpits through the cuffs of her summer shirt. She was quiet, and always sat in a corner of the classroom chatting with the equally well-behaved Igarashi and Sasaki, or otherwise absorbed in a book alone at her desk.

Along with Aki and Miho, I was one of the more "clued-in" girls. I was often told by classmates that I was clued in, and Aki and Miho apparently didn't doubt that they were too, but what did that even mean? Clued in to what? Did it mean looking more grown up than other classmates, or knowing a lot about fashion and makeup and going out with a senior high school boy the way Aki did, or going out for drives until late with a university student home tutor like Miho did? I couldn't help thinking it was a bit of a childish word.

Going by these standards, probably the most clued in of us all in our class would actually be Shiho. Shiho had had a boyfriend since first grade, had kissed him in the fourth grade, and had initiated sex with him in the summer of their first year of junior high. But that wasn't why I thought she was grown up. Even if she hadn't had those experiences, I would have thought the same thing. It was because she wasn't interested in being "clued in" like everyone else. She never used other people's words or sense of values in talking about her own body or her desires. And she always approached her body with the utmost care. This was what I admired most in her.

The first time I heard Shiho talk about sex was in the winter of our first year in junior high.

After school, Shiho and I often found ourselves alone together in the art room. The art club was divided into two sections, oil painting and watercolors, and we were the only two who used oils. The materials were expensive, and working with oils looked difficult, so everyone else chose watercolors, busying themselves with that in art room 2. It was a bit awkward with just the two of us in art room 1, painting in silence, so I struck up a conversation with Shiho, and we gradually became good friends.

She was always well-behaved and serious, just the way she was in our homeroom, and whatever the topic of conversation, she never made fun of me and always carefully considered her answers, so I enjoyed talking with her. Soon after the end of the first winter vacation, we'd been talking about falling in love, and I'd been really surprised to hear that she'd already had sex with a boy. I thought having that experience in the first year of junior high was a bit early, even for the more grown-up girls who played around a lot, and at first I found it hard to believe that such a well-behaved little girl could have done so. My first

SAYAKA MURATA

thought was that she must have been taken advantage of by some pervert with a Lolita fetish.

"No, it's nothing like that. I had sex with my boyfriend of my own free will. So it's all okay."

"What? But how old is your boyfriend? Isn't he taking advantage of you?"

"He's the same age as me. He's my cousin. I started it, both when we first kissed and when we had sex. Of course I didn't do anything that would frighten Yota—oh, that's his name, by the way."

"You started it? But why?"

"Mmm, it's hard to explain, but . . . well, I didn't really think of what we were doing as sex. We were cuddling, and I just wanted to get inside his skin. That's all."

I gazed in disbelief at Shiho's immature body. She didn't even look like she'd started her period yet! After a while, though, listening to her talk, I began to realize that she hadn't done it just to go along with the boy's sexual desire, nor from curiosity, nor from any self-awareness of wanting to be more grown up than those around her, but from pure sexual arousal.

Shiho and her boyfriend could meet only once a year during the summer Obon festival. Every year, all her relatives gathered at the family home in the mountains, and the ten or so cousins spent their time playing with fireworks, eating watermelon, and so on. Shiho and Yota had made a promise when they were little that they would marry

114

each other, and during these summers they would secretly slip out of the house and go exploring in the traditional old storehouse and walk along the paths between their grandmother's rice fields, holding hands.

Shiho lived in Tokyo, whereas the boy lived near their grandmother's house, and at such a distance, it was difficult for them to meet up alone, so during Obon, they spent as much time together as possible. When they were in fourth grade, they'd kissed for the first time, in an attic room of the house, and last year they'd had sex in the storehouse. I was astonished by the way she talked about it all so casually.

I'd always thought kissing and sex was a bit gross. But listening to Shiho, I began to think it was something innocent and pure.

When we were in second grade, Aki from my group and a girl from the classroom next to ours started going on about how they'd been kissed by older boys, and things like that, but to me, the kisses they'd experienced didn't sound anything like what Shiho was talking about.

Wanting to get inside someone's skin. That sort of thing had never even occurred to me. The other girls didn't look like they were kissing boys out of any particular desire of their own. It was more like they wanted to prove to themselves that, having been subjected to a kiss, they were all clued in and grown up.

Shiho had never once said that she had "been kissed." For her, kissing was something she did of her own volition.

If adults heard the sorts of things that Shiho was saying, there would no doubt be a huge scandal, but I thought she was just being true to her own body. She looked carefully at her own desire, and after seeing what her body wanted and respecting her partner's wishes, she had sex. Shiho's kisses were not something lewd created by someone else, but something all her own.

I was not so immature that I thought experiencing sex early would make me grown up. I just wanted to be true to my own sexual arousal in the way that Shiho was.

The weather was clear, without a cloud in the sky, and the watercolor art group had all gone with the teacher to sketch at a local park. With nobody at all left in art room 2 next door, things were quieter than usual.

"Hey, Shiho, when you kiss, do you use your tongue too?" I blurted out as I mixed together some red paint.

Her brush paused, and she laughed.

"Ruri, where did you hear something like that?"

"Yesterday, from Miho and Aki," I said in a small voice, feeling terribly childish.

The only things I knew about kissing and sex were what I'd learned in our health education class. Maybe because of Shiho's influence, I didn't really like people talking about that sort of thing, using vulgar language, and I tended to walk away from the group when they started this kind of talk. "Ruri really hates it when we talk dirty," Aki and the others would say.

I generally ignored anyone who said *Hey, Ruri, did you know* . . . and tried to force me to listen to something dirty, which was probably why I hadn't actually known until yesterday that tongues were involved in kissing. Aki, Miho, and the others burst out laughing. "What, Ruri, didn't you even know that?"

"The way you use your tongue too, there are lots of different techniques, you know!"

"That senior student was about to do it to me, but I got creeped out and ran away. He's really cool, but he does act like he's in a porn movie sometimes."

"Right! Remember that movie we watched online at your house the other day, Aki? It was so sexy!"

It felt quite dangerous hearing the two of them. They probably knew a lot more extreme stuff than Shiho did.

But Aki and Miho and the others were only repeating other people's lewd words. I couldn't help feeling that they were not properly nurturing the lust in their own bodies, which meant they were easily drawn into other people's lewdness. But shouldn't I know about these sorts of things at my age? Mom always told me that sex education was important. "If you didn't know anything, you wouldn't be able to defend yourself," she said. So I had gone to class, but that didn't tell me anything about the "dirty" side of things, and it seemed there was plenty of that out there.

"Is it weird not knowing that sort of thing?" I asked Shiho.

"No, it isn't weird. And what's more, you don't know until the moment comes what sort of kiss you're going to do. When Yota and I kissed, we had no idea that adults did that sort of thing. It's just that it happened to coincide with something I'd thought I wanted to try."

"So it's not that you knew how to kiss when you did it?"

Shiho shook her head and smiled. "No. The two of us just made it up by ourselves. When I later read in a book about other people doing it, I felt a bit relieved, but also a bit disappointed. I thought Yota and I had invented it!"

"Don't you know why you wanted to do it, Shiho?"

"Nope. We started out licking each other's cheeks 'cos they looked so soft and juicy. And then I wanted to get inside Yota's body. I wanted to go inside his skin, and I licked his eyelid. Yota was so surprised, his mouth dropped open, so I stuck my tongue in it. Yota was really shocked, but when I explained it to him, he understood. And he told me to go ahead.

"Yota's skin is suntanned, and thicker than mine. I liked touching it with my tongue, but it was different inside his mouth. First I licked the inside of his lower lip. It was so soft, like a baby, and I was amazed by how soft the internal parts of people's bodies are.

"I wanted to taste more of Yota's insides, and when I flicked my tongue across the back of his teeth, I tasted a little blood. There was a mouth ulcer, a little hole in Yota. I softly licked it with my tongue, taking care not to hurt him. The inside of his body is so complex, and however much I touched it with my tongue, I never got tired of it. Tons of water kept welling up from inside him, making the inside of his mouth wet. His gums were hard, and his veins formed ridges at the root of his tongue. I felt so happy at the thought that I was among his innards!

"I never knew that the inside of Yota's strong body was so soft, and I kept licking the inside of his cheek. He laughed, saying it tickled."

This sounded very different from the "hot kiss techniques" Aki and Miho talked about.

"I wonder if I'll ever feel that way about someone."

"I'm sure you will! You're so grown up, Ruri."

I was taken aback. "What? But Aki and the others say I'm a child. They say I don't know anything."

"I think the only reason you don't know, Ruri, is that you cherish your ignorance. I think it's important to be able to talk properly about dirty things, but maybe it's enough to do so with people who are important to you. I've only ever spoken about this with Yota and you, for example.

Somehow I get the feeling that if you talk too much about it, you might know how to kiss, but you'll no longer be able to kiss your own way. It's not that you don't want to know, Ruri, it's that you want to be free, isn't it?"

I felt better for hearing her say that. Feeling a bit nervous, I swallowed some saliva and said quietly, "Um . . . there's something I haven't told you, Shiho. A long time ago, just once, I had a dream."

"A dream?"

"A strange dream. I was in grade five of elementary school, and I'd just got my first period a little while before. I was asleep in bed, enveloped in my duvet, which smelled of the sun after Mom had aired it outside. And I had a dream of floating lightly in soap bubbles."

Shiho was watching me intently. Normally she never stopped painting when we talked, but today she put her brush down on her palette.

"I started feeling kind of wiggly, and then suddenly all the soap bubbles burst at once. And it felt as though all the veins in my body constricted, as if something inside my body had actually burst too. I was so surprised, I woke up. It was only a dream, but I felt a kind of numb sensation all over, and really refreshed. I still wonder what it was! I tried looking it up in books in the library, but I couldn't find anything about it."

Shiho thought a moment, then said, "I think it was probably what boys call a wet dream."

120

"A wet dream? Do girls have them too?"

"So I've heard. I think I read about it in a novel. It sounds like a wonderful experience!"

"Haven't you ever experienced it, Shiho?"

She shook her head. "I've done it by myself, so I've had that feeling of your body bursting. But I've never had it in a dream."

"Oh." Mixing the red paint on my palette, I asked her, "What does it feel like to do it by yourself? If you don't mind me asking."

"I don't mind you asking me, Ruri. Um . . . it feels like you're doing something really pure."

"Pure?"

"I can't explain it very well, but it's kind of like your body becomes innocent, like a child, and starts feeling nice, and then something bursts in your body. Afterward you feel pleasantly tired and floaty, kind of relieved, and you get sleepy."

What Shiho was saying sounded quite similar to my experience, but it also sounded amazing, like something in a fairy tale.

We heard the teacher's footsteps outside and hastily picked up our brushes.

Shiho got on with painting a rural scene from a photo she'd taken in the summer. I was having trouble painting the plastic apple set on a table, and I carried on mixing the red paint on my palette.

* * *

When I came back from swimming in the school pool, the classroom always felt more humid than ever, and I sometimes had the illusion I was still swimming.

I'd let my hair down so it would dry. My hair was black and reached almost to my waist. It smelled faintly of chlorine from the pool water.

The fourth period was self-study English.

I was half asleep, feeling languid and floaty, listening abstractedly to Aki and Miho chatting playfully with some boys as they filled in the worksheets.

Suddenly one of the boys, a loudmouth called Okazaki, said, "Hey, do girls play solo?"

"Solo play? Ha ha ha! You're crazy, Okazaki!"

All the boys roared with laughter at Okazaki imitating masturbation with his hand.

Grinning, he went on mischievously, "I mean, they all do in porn movies, don't they?"

"Okazaki, you're disgusting! Of course we don't," Aki said loudly, her face bright red, then rolled up her English worksheet and hit him on the back with it.

"I guess. But you know what? I bet Seto has. Maybe her boyfriend taught her or something."

"Yeah, Seto's really sexy!"

Hearing my surname come up so suddenly made my ears burn. Normally I would have yelled back at him, but the conversation I'd had with Shiho the day before replayed in my head, and I couldn't move.

Had the boys heard about that conversation from someone and been laughing about it behind my back? Was that why they were talking about it now, teasing me for being a slut, enjoying seeing my reaction? Just the thought of it made me want to run away.

I couldn't speak and was hoping they'd drop it, when I heard a small voice say "Okazaki-kun."

Okazaki, who was sitting on his desk with his knees up, turned around to see Shiho's small figure standing there.

"Okazaki-kun, here's the class log. The teacher just gave it to me. You were on class duty yesterday, weren't you? The teacher said you should rewrite it."

"Oh, er . . ."

The boys who had all been getting into the dirty talk seemed somewhat stunned by the sudden appearance of childlike Shiho.

She took a deep breath and, still holding out the class log to Okazaki, muttered in a small, feeble voice, as if chanting something, "Our pleasure is ours, your pleasure is yours, we discover our own pleasure, and we don't betray our own pleasure, we don't betray our own bodies . . ."

She was muttering tonelessly and fast, not really intending to be heard. It sounded more like a spell. The black file containing the class log that she was clutching looked like some kind of magic book.

Shiho never normally talked to boys, and everyone looked as though they hadn't managed to catch her words. "Eh? What? What did she say?" They all looked at one another in confusion.

For some reason, I'd clearly heard what she said. She didn't repeat it, just smiled and, looking down, handed the class log to Okazaki, went back to her desk, and started doing the English worksheet.

"Hey, what did she say? Did you hear?"

"No, I didn't. I wonder what it was . . . something about you guys . . . and bodies . . . I kind of heard something, but . . ."

"I don't know, but wasn't it basically something like telling you to stop talking dirty? Hey, Okazaki, you even got told off by little Hashimoto, you idiot!"

"It's true," Aki said, laughing. "Boys always go on and on about things like that. You even made Ruri embarrassed, didn't you?"

Relieved, everyone started up again with the dirty talk.

They all vied with each other to be as slangy and vulgar as possible as they displayed their knowledge and experience. Aki and Miho kept gleefully screeching "No way!" and "You're so disgusting!" and everyone burst out laughing. They were all starting to laugh at their own sexuality.

Shiho never did anything like that. I stared at her, intently completing her English worksheet without looking up.

At lunchtime, as everyone took out their lunch boxes, I grabbed Shiho's arm as she started to stand up, and I pulled her onto the balcony.

"Ruri, what's wrong?" she said. "It's time to have lunch!"

I closed the door behind us so the two of us were alone. Shiho looked mystified.

"Shiho. Um, just now I felt embarrassed about myself. And that made me feel really, really ashamed. So I was super glad when you intervened."

Shiho looked relieved, and her expression relaxed. "You know, me too. I felt somehow that it was me they were laughing at, like they were turning something really important to me into a laughing matter, and I worried that it would be destroyed as a result. So I said those magic words. My voice is really quiet, so I didn't think Okazaki and the others would hear what I said, but I wanted to say it out loud all the same. I had to prove to myself that I could say it, that deep down I didn't feel embarrassed, in order to dispel my own fears. It's a magic charm to protect my world."

Distressed, she kept looking at the floor. "If I hadn't done it, I felt like I could be swallowed up. Same as you, too, Ruri."

Seeing her in her oversize uniform, her face down-turned, that same Shiho I'd always thought of as being so grown up now looked terribly frail. I couldn't help wrapping my arms around her small body.

She was slight, much smaller than I am, and was completely enveloped by my hug. Burying her face in my chest, she said in a confused voice, "What's the matter, Ruri?"

My hair tangled with hers as I hugged her. The water from the pool had evaporated, leaving just a hint of chlorine.

Hugging her boyish body that had yet to mature into womanly curves, I whispered, "Shiho, thank you."

We were still in danger of being easily knocked back by strong words or diminished by the values created by the adults who ruled the world. Each time, we had to make our bodies our own by chanting that magic charm. It was really tiring, but if we didn't protect ourselves like that, our precious world would be destroyed. I hugged Shiho even tighter and said in a bright voice, "Listen to the cicadas. It'll be summer vacation soon!"

She immediately brightened and jumped in my arms. "That's right! It'll be here soon. Can't wait!"

She would be going to the mountains this summer and would meet her boyfriend there. And she would have sex with the boy she really loved. Feeling happy for her, I buried my face in her soft hair.

That night, after getting home from the art club, I took off my uniform and crawled into bed.

Mom would be staying late at her part-time job, and my dinner was on the table, covered in plastic wrap. I was hungry, but there was something I wanted to try first. I wanted to see whether I could make the phenomenon of that dream happen by myself.

I closed my eyes and recalled the dream. I visualized the soap bubbles I'd seen in the dream, and as if responding to the memory, something stirred within my body.

I listened to my body's voice and touched the skin over the responding cells—my Achilles tendon, behind my earlobes, under my knees, the veins in my neck. Little by little the cells began vibrating, and particles, fizzing as though made from stardust, started moving around my body.

I wrapped my right foot in the blanket and pulled it tight. The bits of stardust vibrated and shone and swayed, gradually swelling in time with the movements of my foot.

I was floating inside my own skin. I'd thought that only my blood and inner organs existed in my body. It had never occurred to me that anything like this magical stardust could emerge, and it was the first time in my life that I'd ever realized that there was such a large expanse inside me.

The moment I felt I was about to explode, the particles of light inside me burst, and magical particles instantly evaporated from my entire body. Wondering whether I could see them flying out of me, I opened my eyes a crack and saw my curtain swaying in the night breeze.

The night smells were making the air in my room slowly sway. My hair, strewn over the sheet, was coarser than usual, and I vaguely remembered that I'd been swimming in the pool.

The same pleasant fatigue I'd felt after swimming enveloped my body. I surrendered to the languid feeling of floating and fluttering in the breeze, starting to feel drowsy.

Suddenly looking at my fingertip, I noticed that some of the red paint I'd used when painting after school had stuck to the nail of my thumb, like a childish manicure I'd given myself. I stared at it as I slowly fell into sleep.

Lover on the Breeze

Naoko calls me Puff, because I puff up in the wind and billow in the breeze.

She was in her first year at elementary school when her father, Takashi, hung me in her bedroom. Once he had fixed me in place with silver hooks, he stroked her head in satisfaction.

"Naoko, it's light blue—your favorite color. Isn't it pretty?"

"I wanted pink—blue's for boys." Naoko pouted, but she couldn't take her eyes off my ever so pale, liquid-sky blue.

My role was to cover the right side of her bedroom window.

Outside, a white-painted veranda overlooked the garden beyond. The other cloth, my twin, said dismissively, "Now we're stuck here, we'll just get dirty in the wind," and went to sleep. I wasn't at all sleepy, and I gazed curiously around Naoko's bedroom at the pink cushions and her shiny study desk. As if aware that I alone was awake, Naoko looked over at me. That's when she named me Puff.

Come morning, Naoko went off to school, her red schoolbag on her back. Sometime later, her mother, Kazumi, came in to clean the room. "Let's get some air in here," she said, coming over to open the glass window behind me. For the rest of the day, until Naoko came home, I floated and flapped, almost swimming around the room.

When Naoko came home, she exclaimed, "It's cold in here!" and shut the window. And, still with her schoolbag on her back, she said, "Puff, I'm back," and buried her face deep in my folds.

Despite my name, I hated the wind. In winter it was cold, and in summer it was unpleasantly warm, and the sensation of being touched up all over my body was gross. Naoko always felt the cold and kept the window shut, for which I was thankful.

At night she would quietly bundle me up in her arms and nestle her face up close.

There in the darkened room, I would be caught in her embrace, listening as she murmured my name. Whenever she was sad, she always came to me for a cuddle.

Yukio first came to her room around the time I had just turned eleven. It was the season I hated most, when strong, gusty wind whipped up petals from the cherry tree in the garden and stuck them all over me.

Naoko had just started her second year in high school. Kazumi was jittery, and she kept coming up to the room with juice or snacks. Every time she went out again, Naoko and Yukio looked at each other and giggled shyly.

"Sorry," Naoko said. "It's the first time I've ever had a boy come to my room, so Mom's getting a bit carried away."

"That's okay."

Yukio was a rather slight, unremarkable-looking boy. He wasn't all that tall, either, and his face, with its beautifully pronounced cheekbones, was smaller than Naoko's.

The surface of his fine black hair shone pale brown in the sunlight streaming through the window. Beneath thin, delicate brows, his eyes were shaped like small leaves, the black pupils reflecting soft brown in the sunlight.

His long arms, extending from the rolled-up sleeves of the white shirt of his uniform, were thin, but the muscles were well defined, contrasting with Naoko's soft limbs.

Yukio was a little taller than Kazumi, and as he walked, he generated a slight breeze in the room.

"Oh, Puff's got caught in the window." Naoko got up, opened the window, and pulled me loose.

"Puff?"

"This curtain . . . that's what I used to call it when I was little, and the habit's stuck. I suppose you think that's very childish."

"Uh-uh."

Yukio didn't laugh at Naoko, just shook his head, narrowing his eyes.

"It's a good name," he said simply, and bit into one of the cookies Kazumi had left for them.

Every time his fingers and arms moved, soundlessly, a light breeze blew through the room. It was as if his sinewy limbs were summoning it.

As I watched those quiet arms gently making the air vibrate, it occurred to me that I wanted to feel this breeze flow all over me.

Yukio often came to the house after that. On his sixth visit, the two of them were watching a movie on the small television in the corner of the room when Naoko suddenly tugged at the sleeve of his uniform.

Yukio swayed as though in the breeze and brought his face close to Naoko's, lightly placing a kiss on her. His thin, pale pink lips fluttered down toward her without a sound. They reminded me of the falling cherry blossom petals as they stuck to the window screen.

Yukio's eyes were open, his lashes just slightly lowered. Naoko had her eyes firmly closed, so I alone noticed how his lashes fluttered in the breeze.

One Saturday night not long afterward, Yukio stayed over at the house. Kazumi and Takashi were attending a memorial service some distance away.

Laughter sounded continually from downstairs as the pair of them cooked dinner, and the aroma of stew came wafting up to the second floor.

Later they came upstairs and sat side by side eating milk pudding. Naoko had apparently made it the night before and had left it to chill overnight. The soft white custard slipped easily between Yukio's pale blossom-pink lips.

"This is good." Yukio looked at Naoko, smiling.

Naoko pouted unhappily. "But the potato salad was a disaster, and you cooked the stew pretty much all on your own."

"It's the least I can do when you're letting me stay over."

"No way! And anyone can make milk pudding."

"But it tastes great!"

"But . . ."

After finishing their dessert, Yukio and Naoko stood up and slipped between the white sheets on the bed. I watched intently as his inexpert fingers slipped over her skin and, though he rarely perspired, beads of moisture welled up on his forehead.

Just as a small drop fell from his delicate skin and landed on her collarbone, I noticed her glance over at me.

The next morning, Naoko got out of bed alone, dressed, and went downstairs.

A faint smell of eggs frying came wafting up. It seemed she was getting her own back for yesterday by cooking breakfast for Yukio.

Yukio remained asleep, his shoulder exposed, in the bed she had vacated.

His bony shoulder shivered with cold, and at that moment I slipped one of my silver hooks from the curtain rail.

One by one, my silver hooks slipped free, and as a gust of the wind that I hated so much came blowing through the window, I jumped and let myself be carried on it.

I swam through the room on the wind. It all happened in a moment, soundlessly, as if on the ocean floor. Holding my breath, I quietly let myself down over Yukio's body.

I could feel that skin I had been watching for so long.

"Naoko . . ." murmured Yukio in his sleep, drawing me into an embrace.

A light breeze as he raised his arms set my body atremble. Every movement of his fingers or legs or shoulders generated a quiet, slightly damp puff of air.

"Naoko."

Again a light breeze came from his lips.

Each time it blew, I breathed it in, trembling. I finally realized I had been hanging in this room for the past eleven years just in order to be bathed in this breeze.

*   *   *

"What's going on?"

Naoko's voice was suddenly harsh. She must have finished making breakfast, for she now stood by the door in semidarkness, staring at us.

"What the—" Yukio sat up, rubbing his eyes.

"What is Puff doing over here?"

"I don't know. He must have blown over in the wind."

"As if! You're telling me he unhooked himself from the rail?"

"I don't know how that happened."

Yukio looked at me, puzzled. The bed creaked under his weight, and the tremor caused me to slip to the floor with a faint rustle.

That winter, Naoko and friends from her school club gathered for a small Christmas party in her room. The room was littered with alcopop cans and snack packets.

One brown-haired boy who was sitting in the center of the room telling joke after joke suddenly tapped Yukio on the shoulder.

"Hey, Yukio, have you ever been unfaithful?"

"Of course not."

"You've never done it with another girl? Not even once?"

A short-haired girl who was a close friend of Naoko's said, "Stupid! Yukio's not like you," and slapped him on the head.

Watching them as he sipped his fizzy drink, Yukio said innocently, "Actually, there may have been one time . . ."

"Eh? Really? You never!" exclaimed the girl, drawing closer.

Yukio laughed, then abruptly looked over and pointed at me.

"Just once, I mistook Puff for Naoko."

"Whaaat?" Everyone laughed.

"I cuddled him and called him Naoko. It really came as a shock when I realized what I was doing!"

"Yukio, you're so dumb!"

The brown-haired boy alone seemed mystified. "Who's Puff?"

"It's Naoko's pet name for her curtain, like it's a teddy bear or something. 'Cos she's still just a kid."

"Hah! I bet you find that sort of thing cute, don't you, Yukio?"

Yukio chuckled quietly and poured some more fizzy drink between his lips.

Only Naoko didn't laugh. She sat huddled in the corner of her bed and glared at me.

One afternoon not long afterward, still in their school uniforms, Yukio and Naoko sat talking quietly in her room, which was filled with evening sunlight.

"You want to split up? Why?"

I was taken aback when Yukio said this, and I trembled even though the window wasn't open.

"Um . . ."

"Won't you give me a reason?"

"Well . . . I'm in love with someone else," said Naoko, staring into space, her eyes dry. "To tell the truth, I've known about it ever since we got together. You reminded me of him, and that's why I fell for you. I'm sorry."

"Oh."

Yukio nodded meekly and looked sad. They sat in silence for a while, staring at the sky changing color outside the window, as though watching a movie. The sunset gradually darkened and finally turned to indigo.

Yukio wept a little.

I watched the transparent drops trickling from his eyes, and for the first time, I hated Naoko for making him cry like that.

There, in the room vacated by Yukio, Naoko embraced me. It was the first time in a very long time, and her knees trembled as they sank into the carpet. Her hands gripped me tightly and wouldn't let go.

Naoko's unnaturally hot breath felt oppressive, like a gust of summer wind. She made me damp with her breath as she buried her face in me.

Motionless, she closed her eyes as if in prayer.

There, in that room void of the breeze aroused by Yukio's arms and fingers, my body hung heavily. The indigo-tinged air stiffened in the silence, no longer making any attempt to move.

Puzzle

Sanae slipped into the packed train carriage, as though drawn in by the warm, damp air that spilled out through the doors when they shook open. She slowly sank her body into the wall of passengers, pressured from behind by more office workers pushing their way on after her. She snuggled under a salaryman's chin, and his damp breath tickled her forehead.

"Are you okay, Sanae?" asked her colleague Emiko, wedged in next to her.

Sanae crinkled her eyes in a smile. "I'm fine!"

As the train moved off, the passengers all raised their faces slightly, as if seeking oxygen.

Surrounded by lips facing upward, Sanae relaxed her body and leaned into the eddy of body heat. Submerged in air full of sighs released from numerous mouths, she closed her eyes and savored the dampness on her skin, floating in it, happy being smothered in the carbon dioxide spewed out by passengers. Long ago the term *forest bathing* had been popular, but Sanae preferred "people bathing" like this.

Even more people got on at the next stop, and enthralled by the mounting warm pressure, she opened her eyes a little and noticed the salaryman next to her cluck his tongue. She stared almost enviously at the black hole in his face, fancying that she could see through the thin, cracked lips to the red-black tongue bouncing against the inside of his mouth. Feeling her gaze on him, the salaryman looked briefly puzzled, but when he saw her smiling slightly, he seemed to understand that her look was appreciative, and his expression changed to one of pride.

The train pulled into the station where Sanae had to transfer, and she reluctantly joined the flow of passengers getting off. Emiko was on the platform, smoothing down her tousled hair with a sigh.

"Emiko."

"Oh, Sanae, am I glad to see you! I thought we'd lost each other. Today's rush hour is just the worst, isn't it? I really can't stand it!" Emiko frowned grumpily, then noticed that Sanae was smiling and looked at her, puzzled. "You don't look fazed at all, Sanae. You're always like that. You never get irritable, do you?"

"You hate the rush hour, don't you, Emiko?"

"Nobody likes it when it's packed like that!"

"Really? Actually, I've never felt that way myself."

Seeing Sanae gazing at the noisy wave of people, her expression still soft, Emiko shrugged. "You have an air about you, Sanae, as if you see life from above the clouds. I've never seen you get annoyed about anything. The younger girls were saying the same thing, that you're always so kind and never, ever get angry."

"Really?"

"Yes, especially Yuka. She's always going on and on about how much she likes you. She wants to go out drinking with you again."

"Yuka likes everyone, though!"

As they got on the escalator, chatting, the next train slid into the platform. Sanae turned in the direction of the sound and looked down on the eddy of living organisms flowing out through the doors, almost reaching out a hand toward them.

"Anything wrong, Sanae?"

"Oh, no, nothing." Sanae shook her head lightly and turned back to face Emiko. Behind her, the noise coming from the heat and physical presence of the living organisms made the air tremble as it slowly came pressing up behind her.

Sanae lived in a trim little apartment building crammed into a small space in a major office district. As she walked in her high heels between the rows of buildings, she couldn't shake the sensation that she, too, was one of these buildings.

Gazing at the gradations of gray concrete, she recalled the public housing project she'd lived in as a child. Ever since she could remember, she had felt that she was one of the blocks in that project.

She'd always been on the frail side and had often sat on a bench in the project's park, watching the other children playing. When she handed back a ball that came rolling up to her feet, she had been surprised by the heat in another child's hands. The sensation of living flesh was utterly unlike her own pale hands. They were living organisms, and the core of life was firmly embedded inside them, she'd thought at the time. Behind her back, the gray project buildings stood in rows, watching the children in the same way that she was.

When she left home and came to live alone in Tokyo, this office district had been recommended to her because it was so convenient for transport lines. The sight of it somehow made her feel that being here had to be her destiny. Ah, this is how the ugly duckling—the baby swan mistakenly raised by ducks—must have felt when it returned to its own flock, she thought. Yet, unlike in the picture book, Sanae wasn't returning to a flock of swans, but to rows of inorganic buildings. Although the flock of humans she had mistakenly blended with was far more beautiful, before she knew it, she was being pushed back by nature to where she belonged.

Through a gap in the curtains in her apartment she looked down on the heads and backs of people passing by below the streetlamps. She never got tired of watching people moving around, no matter how long she spent doing it.

The core of life was embedded within people. How beautiful living organisms were! She diligently followed their skin and muscles with her eyes, as though looking at precious cells through a microscope.

Inside the body, squirming organs were densely crammed within a faintly transparent skin. Around them stretched the muscles, like roots, and blood was constantly circulating in the veins that stood out on the neck. Unconsciously, Sanae slipped her face through the gap in the curtain and pressed her forehead to the window to stare at them, but then someone looked at her, as if aware they were being watched. Hastily she left the window and took refuge inside the darkened room.

She saw her pale face reflected in a small hand mirror lying on the low table. She'd forgotten to turn it over that morning, she thought, reaching out a hand for it.

The surface of her face reflected in it was somewhat pasty, and it was impossible to see anything of the blood and flesh that must lie within. Her cheeks and forehead were such a uniform color that she began to wonder whether her insides were filled with the same materials as the surface. Only the eye shadow painted on her eyelid had a faint luster, which made it look all the more like white concrete painted over in one spot.

Recalling the lukewarm carbon dioxide from numerous mouths showering her in the train, Sanae breathed deeply as she gazed into the mirror. But the breeze coming out through the gap between her enamel-coated teeth was cold, as though she were simply blowing air, not breathing.

Sanae sighed, turned the mirror over, and placed it back on the table. She didn't want to look at herself, as she barely resembled any kind of life-form, so she'd decided never to look in the mirror except when she was getting ready for work in the morning. There was no mirror in her tiny bathroom, and this one small hand mirror was the only one in her apartment. Feeling a little better now that she could no longer see her own appearance, she got up and started preparing her dinner.

It was in her nature to never feel very hungry. She always felt that she was just pouring food into the black hole in her face, as though she were merely a garbage bin for kitchen waste. That felt gross, so she tried taking only nutritional supplements, but then she'd fainted from anemia and since then had forced herself to chuck a certain amount of food into her face hole.

Steam smelling of dashi and miso wafted up as she reheated the soup she'd made that morning. Yet even inhaling that fragrance did not stimulate her appetite, and not knowing what to do, she kept stirring the soup with the silver ladle.

* * *

During her lunch break at work the next day, Sanae joined several colleagues in an empty meeting room. Normally they each brought packed lunches they'd either made themselves or bought in a convenience store, but today everyone had the same yellow plastic bags lined up on the table. That morning they'd all gone together to a new bento shop opened nearby. The place sold unusual types of bento, such as taco rice and loco moco, and had a good reputation, so they'd decided to buy lunch there today.

Unwrapping her bento, Emiko pursed her lips. "I was really pissed at that guy in the store. He was so rude!"

"It's true, he was. They should fire him—he's only a casual worker. Shall we phone in to make a complaint?"

Everyone seemed irritated by how curt the worker who had taken their orders had been.

One girl scooped up some taco rice in a plastic spoon and put it in her mouth, then grimaced and said, "Yuck, this is disgusting."

"Right—it's not just the attitude, the food tastes awful. It's just the worst. I won't be going back there again."

"Yeah, we should have stuck with our normal lunches."

The meat was dry, and the sauce too strong. It didn't exactly taste like it was a high-quality product.

Sanae was smiling as she savored her food, and Emiko said to her, "Aren't you annoyed about that bento place, Sanae?"

"Me? No, not really," she replied with a smile, and another friend laughed.

"You're so bighearted, Sanae. You hardly ever get angry."

"I don't think that's really true, though," Sanae said.

"Oh, it is. Just today Okajima was saying all kinds of things to you, but you didn't even pull a face."

Okajima, a woman in the same section as Sanae, was known for admonishing workers in a pretty severe tone and was generally disliked, but Sanae had never gotten annoyed with her even once.

"She probably has a point, but it's the way she says it! It makes me not want to listen, really. It just gets right up my nose."

"I hate Okajima too. I'm glad I'm not in the same section as her."

"Well, nobody likes her! You poor thing, Sanae."

"But, see, you don't seem to have a problem with her, Sanae. I've never heard you bad-mouth her, and you don't seem to be merely putting up with her either."

"You really don't hate anyone, do you, Sanae?"

"Not really." Sanae shook her head and smiled. Toward life-forms, all she had was a yearning that left no room for hatred.

"You're incredible, Sanae. The way you can say that without being sarcastic!"

"You think?"

"I really hate people who say they don't hate anyone, 'cos they're hypocrites, but not you, Sanae. I get the feeling that you mean it."

Sanae picked up her bottle of mineral water from the table. "I've never felt particularly irritated by anyone, ever since I was little."

"Really? I guess you have to be born that way. Myself, I'm annoyed all the time. My skin even gets dry from stress. How lucky you are."

"No, I'm not lucky at all!" Sanae said, emotion in her voice. She was the one who always envied the other women!

She could see the reflection of light on the saliva inside the girl's mouth when she sighed. Life-forms were a spring from which all kinds of fluids gushed forth. Saliva was one, and urine and blood and other liquids, and around them hung the rank smell of air permeated with the stench of inner organs that erupted from the mouth. Each of those things was totally lifeless when emitted by Sanae, however.

Sanae gazed steadily at the girl, who now peered back into her eyes.

"What lovely eyes you have, Sanae. You can see in them how much you like people."

"That's true. Whenever you look at me, I feel good."

Embarrassed to realize that she'd been staring at the girl, Sanae looked down.

She couldn't help staring at the life-forms, to the extent that it might be considered rude, but somehow they didn't dislike it. They all probably sensed that the gaze she fixed them with was tinged with envy. Sanae's gaze was always received amicably.

She had finished her meal and was just about to clear it away and go back to work when Emiko spoke to her.

"Oh, I almost forgot. Sanae, I brought this for you."

"You did?" She took the thin plastic bag. Inside was a plastic case.

"I've finished with it, so I thought I'd give it to you."

"What is it? Music?"

"No. It's an exercise DVD. You mentioned that your body felt cold, didn't you? This is pretty strenuous exercise, so I thought it'd be effective for poor circulation."

What she'd meant about her body being cold was a bit different from what Emiko had understood, but Sanae was glad that she cared, so she smiled.

"Thank you. I'll give it a go."

"No worries. In any case, it was lying around at home. Oh, I'll just pop down to the bathroom before going back to work," Emiko said, waving goodbye as she rushed down the corridor. Sanae quietly gripped the plastic bag in her hand, thinking of all the excrement filling Emiko's body.

As Sanae and Emiko were leaving their office building after work, a man standing next to the flower bed outside the main entrance looked up at them. He was wearing a long-sleeved black shirt, unsuited to the summer sun, with slim-fit pants of the same color, and upon catching Sanae's and Emiko's eyes, he hastily averted his face and began fiddling with the phone in his hand.

"Who's that? He looks shady," Emiko said, making a face.

The man kept his face downturned and repeatedly took his phone out of his pocket and put it back in, but at one point his hand must have slipped as he tried to squeeze the phone into his pants, and he dropped it.

The phone landed near Sanae's feet, and she picked it up and went over to him.

"Here you are," she said with a smile.

Surprise registered on his face as he looked at her, and he grabbed the phone from her and ran off.

"You should have just left it. You're too nice sometimes, Sanae."

Sanae was recalling the sweat oozing from the man's forehead and the eyeballs moving around in the gaps in his skin. Looking down at her own skin, she saw that there was not even a hint of moisture oozing from its pale surface, even in this heat.

"Emiko, if I do those exercises on the DVD you gave me today, will I be able to sweat?"

"Oh, that! It does work, you know. I was soaked after doing it."

"Really?"

A few drops of liquid had formed a stain on the asphalt where the man had been standing. It was probably some of his sweat. Sanae stroked her own still surface and visualized the wriggling flesh within the dripping liquid.

Sanae changed into a thin T-shirt and short pants and switched on the TV. She wanted to try the DVD Emiko had given her as soon as she got home, before even having dinner.

As she placed the DVD in the deck, a foreign woman instructor appeared on the screen. Seeing her body, with its well-defined muscles below the skin, Sanae imagined the muscles stretched within that body and the heart at its center. She almost got carried away, but then the music started and she hastily began moving her body.

After she'd been moving awhile, following the instructions, little by little she felt the contents of her skin undergoing a change. The water inside her body was beginning to ooze out. She even had the sensation that liquid was being forced out through the small pores in the surface of the skin on her forehead.

The sweat oozing from her face didn't stick, however, but smoothly trickled down the surface. Seeing the transparent liquid dripping onto her arm, she was reminded of condensation on a window. It was just water oozing from her body, not a proper bodily fluid. Air was blowing with more force from her mouth, but this made her feel all the more that she was merely a machine that had a switch somewhere.

After continuing this heavy exercise for about an hour, the sensation that she was a receptacle only grew stronger. However much her inner organs raged and moisture oozed heavily out, Sanae felt that she was simply their container.

Finally she finished exercising and switched off the screen with the remote control. All that was reflected on the darkened TV was a small gray building dripping liquid from the condensation on its surface.

Sanae stood there in a daze without wiping away the water that had oozed out from within her. Suddenly something occurred to her, and covering her shirt with her hand, she pressed on the location of her heart. It was beating wildly, but this just gave her the sensation that it wasn't hers, more like a goldfish she'd swallowed that was flapping around inside.

She sighed, moved close to the dark screen, and looked at her face. Her eyes, nose, and mouth had dark holes in them, and she could catch glimpses of her tongue in her mouth. It was like a slug stuck to the window, and she couldn't possibly think that it was flesh with her own nerves running through it.

The next day, there was a company get-together after work, and as Sanae was leaving the office with her friends, Emiko suddenly stopped.

"What's wrong?"

Emiko looked at Sanae and, without saying anything, jerked her chin in the direction of the flower bed. The same man they'd seen the day before was there, gripping a woman by her wrists.

Sanae heard Emiko murmur, "He was lying in wait for Yuka," and she looked again to see that it was her younger colleague Yuka that the man was holding. The girl next to her frowned.

"What *is* that? Is he Yuka's boyfriend? That's a really threatening vibe, though."

"Should we help her?"

"But it looks like serious trouble. Maybe we should get a man to help?"

While they all looked on from a distance, Sanae didn't miss a beat, walking straight over to the couple.

"What's going on, Yuka?"

"Sanae," Yuka said in a feeble voice.

"Hello," Sanae said to the man. "Do you know this girl?"

The man, his shoulders shaking, noticed the friendly smile on Sanae's face and let go of Yuka, as though his strength had drained out of him.

"Is anything wrong?" Sanae's smile grew even friendlier, and the man took a step back, averted his eyes, and walked away, wiping the sweat from his downturned face with his black shirt.

As Sanae sadly watched his departing figure, Yuka gripped hold of her arm.

"Sanae, thank you!"

"You're sweating heavily, Yuka. Are you okay?"

"Yes . . ."

Sanae gazed at the sweat on Yuka's forehead and neck, and smiled.

"Sanae, are you okay?" she heard Emiko say behind her.

"Sure."

"I'm glad you're safe. Well, let's get going then. Quickly!"

"Yes, let's go, Yuka."

Sanae put her arm around Yuka and realized that her back was wet too. Savoring the moisture seeping into her own dry arm, she pressed her arm against Yuka's back.

About an hour after the party started, Sanae saw Yuka shakily stand up from where she was seated farther inside, her face pale. She was grasping her lower chest, as though in pain, and as Sanae rushed to follow her, she imagined the liquid that had probably risen up to that part of her.

As she'd thought, Yuka was crouched down, vomiting into the toilet bowl.

"Are you okay?"

"Sanae . . ."

Yuka weakly gave her an apologetic look, then immediately turned back to the toilet.

It was as though there'd been a lot of water hidden away somewhere in that small body, as multicolored vomit of solids mixed in with liquid flowed into the toilet bowl. Food that had been on the table until a while ago had been dissolved by her internal organs and was giving off a completely different stench.

Impressed, Sanae put her face close to the toilet bowl. It had been less than an hour since the food entered Yuka's mouth, yet it had already dissolved this much! How powerful the internal organs of life-forms were!

Sanae slowly rubbed Yuka's back, hoping she'd vomit some more water smelling of innards. Right on cue, more liquid came welling up out of her lips.

When Sanae unconsciously started rubbing Yuka's back harder, there was a strangled cry, and she came to herself.

"I'm sorry, was I being too rough?" she asked, peering into Yuka's face. "Are you okay?"

"Yeah . . . thanks, Sanae."

It looked as though even more liquid would overflow from Yuka's eyes, which were moist with tears from having vomited repeatedly. Sanae gazed at these holes, entranced by the prospect of yet more liquid coming from them, but Yuka sighed, held her hand over her mouth, and looked down. Sanae took out a handkerchief and wiped away the small specks of vomit from Yuka's chest.

"Oh, you really don't need to do that for me."

"It's okay. When you throw up, it's best to get it all out. Right?"

The smell of vomit and alcohol hung over the toilet bowl. Savoring being enveloped in the odor of bodily fluids permeated with the smell of viscera, Sanae gazed in enchantment at Yuka, who was its source.

"Yes, I'm feeling much better now . . ." Yuka said, and she stood up and flushed the toilet. The rich concoction of bits of battered chicken and fried noodles dissolved in gastric juice was sucked away, and the toilet bowl returned to its insipid state with just clear water. Yuka gargled with tap water and said hoarsely, "I'm sorry, but I'm going home now. I'll pay my share later . . ."

"Okay, I'll go get your things for you." Sanae smiled at her, mesmerized by the faint smell of viscera that hung about Yuka's lips every time she spoke.

She went to get the belongings and put her arm around Yuka's shoulders as she led her outside. Yuka looked up at her with teary eyes.

"Sanae, how come you're so kind to me?"

Sanae tilted her head uncomprehendingly. "What?"

"I vomited such a lot and was in such a disgusting state, yet you kept rubbing my back . . ." Yuka said weakly.

"You're not disgusting at all!" Sanae said with a smile.

"And earlier too, while everyone else was watching from a distance, you came to help me . . ." Yuka went on, tears in her eyes. "That guy was my ex-boyfriend. I broke up with him, but he won't take no for an answer, and he keeps hanging around. I'm actually scared of him."

"Really?"

"Lately he's been lying in wait for me at work, too."

Sanae pictured the man. He'd been acting a bit weirdly, but that had made him look alive. She smiled, recalling his shoulders trembling under his black shirt.

"Well, he might be waiting outside your place, so shall I come with you?"

"I can't possibly put you out any more than I already have. I'll take a taxi to a friend's place. I'll be fine."

"Okay."

Sanae flagged down a taxi and got Yuka settled in the back seat. Yuka bowed her head deeply, holding a handkerchief over her mouth.

"Thank you so much for everything, Sanae. Really."

Sanae watched as the taxi departed, then went back into the restaurant. Emiko and the others came up to her, looking worried.

"How's Yuka? Is she all right?"

"Yes. She seemed to be feeling much better. I just saw her off in a taxi."

"She didn't even last an hour. Maybe she hadn't been feeling well to begin with."

"She appeared to be drinking more than usual."

"Mmmm. She did look as though she was drowning her sorrows, didn't she? It looks like she's caught up in some trouble with that weird man we saw earlier. Thanks for looking after her, Sanae. You always help everyone in trouble. It's so good of you. Well, the night's still young, how about we get back to the party?"

"Sorry, but I need to go to the bathroom first," Sanae said, and headed for the toilet.

Approaching the toilet bowl where Yuka had been crouching, she could still sense the lingering smell of Yuka's viscera. She pulled down her underwear and sat on the toilet, noticing that it was still warm from when Yuka had been clutching it.

Sanae gently took a deep breath and strained her lower abdomen. She wasn't very good at eliminating waste. Even when she wanted to urinate or defecate, it seemed like someone else's business, and she didn't feel any urgency, so she couldn't manage it without straining.

After a while, a warm liquid finally started streaming from her body. Having somehow managed to get it all out, she stood up and turned to look at the toilet bowl. Maybe she'd overdone it with the vitamin supplements, for the liquid was an abnormally vivid yellow, as though paint had been dissolved in it. There was absolutely no hint of a smell of animal body waste coming from it.

However hard she gazed at it, it simply looked like a bucket of yellow paint, and she couldn't detect any trace of a life-form emanating from it.

Nor was there any sensation in her body of feeling refreshed after elimination. It just felt like some of the colored water flowing around her body had left it.

She sighed and flushed the toilet, and the lemon-colored water was sucked away.

She went back to her seat and started gathering her things. "Sorry, but I'm going home too," she told Emiko. "I'm not feeling very well."

"Oh dear, are you drunk too, Sanae? But you hardly drank anything!"

"I feel a bit like I've got a cold coming on. I shouldn't have pushed myself to come tonight."

"Are you okay? Shall I see you home?"

"I've just got a bit of a temperature, I'll be okay. Sorry, but here's my and Yuka's share of the bill. Thanks, Emiko."

Having handed the money to Emiko, Sanae put her thin cardigan over her shoulders and left the restaurant. As she adjusted her bag on her shoulder, she recalled the sweat oozing from the man and the vomit that had spurted from Yuka's mouth.

She took out her handkerchief, which smelled faintly of Yuka's viscera. She stroked her own lips, but only cold air came out. Irritated by the way it wasn't even damp, she pushed her index finger into her mouth. But all that was there was a fluid like rainwater, devoid of any mucus.

She hung her head, eventually managing to take a deep breath and set off at a run through the streets of the nighttime entertainment district.

To begin with, she was just trotting along, but gradually she picked up speed. Water gushed out of her, and oxygen and carbon dioxide began furiously coming and going in her nose and mouth.

Holding her hand to her chest, she could feel her heart beating violently. However, just as the night before, this frenzied heart did not feel like it was her own, and she could only think of it as a separate creature living parasitically off her. The sensation that she was merely a concrete receptacle housing it grew even stronger.

This wasn't going to work, she thought with a little sigh, and stopped running.

Without realizing it, she had been headed for the office district where her company was located, and when she wiped away the body fluid dripping from her face and looked up, she saw standing before her a pale gray office building.

Looking up at it, Sanae gulped despite herself. It was the very image of Sanae herself right now.

She glimpsed flashes of dark red and pale white figures inside its rows of windows. These were the building's innards. She was mesmerized by the wriggling flesh in the windows.

Breathing and pulsing life-forms were moving around inside the rectangular concrete block. It was itself a quiet animal. It wasn't a receptacle in which the creatures lived, but one single large life-form.

Sanae touched her chest. Inside it, her heart was beating, its vibrations reaching her skin.

Concrete and people were not opposites. All the people crawling around in the world were the shared inner organs of all the gray buildings like herself. This was what Sanae was thinking as she unsteadily approached the building.

As she touched the pale gray surface, the cold of the concrete seeped into her. The backs of Sanae's pale, pasty hands looked as though they were blending into the concrete. Yet she no longer felt that they were inorganic matter. Whether it was due to the vibrations of her viscera or from cars passing outside, the surface of the building was quivering slightly. Feeling affection for this building-animal, she kept stroking the concrete with her white hands, slowly savoring its vibrations.

"Are you okay, Sanae?" Hearing Emiko's voice, Sanae came back to herself. "You look really out of it!"

Out of it? Maybe she was, Sanae thought as she returned Emiko's smile.

She was having lunch with her colleagues in the same place as usual—something that had been totally familiar to her until yesterday, but now she felt that she was in a completely different place.

Her friends, who until yesterday had been human, were sitting there right in front of her possessed of an entirely different aspect. They were now a single mass of flesh and blood enclosed in a thin membrane, squirming and pulsing, emitting sounds and giving off heat.

Sanae looked slowly around the room. Within the building's inner walls, she was of one flesh. She looked down at her arms, which seemed somewhat inorganic and incongruous with her surroundings, as if she were a fragment of plastic or an artificial organ that had mistakenly been swallowed up and become part of the building's internal organs. But she didn't feel the sort of alienation she'd felt until yesterday. "I am a small building, so the internal organs before me now are my organs too," she murmured to herself. Whether external walls or internal organs, they were all one single form, one large creature.

"Um, Sanae, has something good happened?" asked one girl, peering into Sanae's pale face. "Did you get a boyfriend maybe?"

"I was thinking the same! It's like gentleness is overflowing from your eyes even more than usual."

"What are you talking about?" Emiko asked, laughing. "But I kind of get what you mean," she added, peering into Sanae's eyes.

"Oh, no. Nothing in particular has happened," Sanae said. "Maybe it's the effect of that DVD you gave me, Emiko."

"Oh that! Did you like it?"

"It was amazing."

"What DVD? A movie?" one girl asked, leaning forward, so Emiko began telling her about the exercises.

In her trance, Sanae watched these two lumps of flesh draw close to each other. Their quivering pale crimson flesh, visible through thin membranes, was so close they might blend into one. With every breath, they faintly expanded and contracted, evidence that they were alive. Yet it wasn't merely evidence of their life, but also of the heartbeat of the large building around them.

Sanae stroked her own dry surface. She could feel the flesh within it, where organs the color of blood were pulsing just like the organs before her eyes. The very thought gave her a rush of affection for her own insides, which until now she'd been convinced were parasitic.

"Oh look, Sanae's smiling again! No way it's that DVD. It's got to be a new boyfriend!"

"Right? Come on, Sanae, you've got to tell us!"

The membrane-covered fleshes all leaned toward her. Sanae laughed out loud in spite of herself. This triggered the internal organs, which also started to give off sounds, their flesh trembling. The sounds they made reverberated around the room, echoing throughout the building.

Leaving work, Sanae was being slowly spewed out of the office building when she noticed the man in the black shirt standing outside. She gave him a friendly smile as she went up to say hello.

The man was taken aback, and his shoulders shook as he looked at her.

"Is something wrong?" she asked.

Beads of sweat rolled down his forehead toward his eyeballs, which were darting here and there, trying to escape from her curious gaze. Sanae took out her handkerchief to wipe away the sweat.

The man hastily averted his face.

"You're getting sweat in your eyes," Sanae told him gently.

He opened his mouth, but then he heard people's voices coming out of the building, and abruptly he ran off.

Sanae was left standing there, clutching the handkerchief in her hand.

Realizing that her cell phone was vibrating inside her bag, she took it out and opened the screen. An email had come from Yuka.

Hi, Sanae. Thank you so much for yesterday. If you're free tomorrow evening, would you mind meeting up somewhere? There's something I'd like to tell you.

Sanae replied that she was free, glanced in the direction where the man had run off, and set off toward the station.

During lunch break the next day, Sanae skipped lunch and instead went to the bathroom, put the lid down on the toilet bowl, and sat on top of it.

She took out a compact mirror and looked in it to see her face there, grayish as ever. It had a number of holes here and there, the inner corners of her eyes, her nostrils and mouth. Peering closely at the corners of her eyes or mouth, she could see within them flesh the color of blood. She had never thought of these things as her own, but now they felt like charming creatures that had slipped inside her.

Did hermit crab shells also think so fondly of the lifeforms that crept inside them? She left the toilet cubicle and was on her way back to her desk when she suddenly stopped in the corridor and looked out the window at the building's entrance below. Little by little, internal organs were spilling out of it. She felt as though she and the building were connected, and that it was her own feet they were leaving through. Maybe the internal organs squirming inside her would similarly flow out and be sucked into other buildings. At night, all the flesh would leave and it would become simply a concrete box standing motionless, waiting for the internal organs to come again the next day.

She could have watched those internal organs outside all day, but suddenly she felt a tap on her back.

"So here you are, Sanae! I was looking for you. I called your phone too."

She turned to see Emiko looking at her with concern.

"I've already had lunch. What have you been doing?"

"I'm sorry, I was just spacing out."

"Sanae, are you okay? The day before yesterday you had a cold, didn't you? If you're not feeling well, you should go home."

"I'm fine! In fact, I'm feeling even better than usual."

Emiko tilted her head slightly and looked at her questioningly.

"Sanae, there's something even more gentle about you lately—I thought so yesterday too. Are you sure you haven't got a boyfriend?"

"No, no, nothing like that."

"Really? Well, never mind. It's just that when you didn't turn up to lunch, everyone was saying that you must be on the phone with your new boyfriend. And that you're such a good person, they sometimes feel a kind of distance from you, but somehow since yesterday it feels like that wall's come down."

"Is that so?"

"Yes, definitely! Well, be sure to give us any good news, okay? Oh look, it's getting late. We don't have time to be chatting here like this. You haven't had lunch yet, have you, Sanae? You'd better hurry up before the lunch break finishes."

"It's okay. I'm not feeling hungry anyway."

"Well, if you're sure. But if you're not feeling well, you mustn't push yourself, okay?" Emiko said to make sure, then added, "I'm going to brush my teeth," gave a little wave, and rushed off to the powder room.

Sanae watched her go, then looked at her own eyes reflected in the window.

Everyone, all the internal organs, took comfort in being showered in tenderness by these eyes. Taking this as proof that they were all one creature, happiness welled up in Sanae. She lightly stroked the wall of the corridor. It felt warmer than usual, as though out of fondness for the internal organs coming and going within it.

Sanae finished work right on time and went into the changing room to find that Yuka had already changed her clothes and was there waiting for her.

"I'm sorry, did I keep you waiting?" Sanae said.

"No problem."

Sanae smiled at Yuka as she took off her uniform. "Where shall we go? Depending on what you want to talk about, maybe it's better not to stay too close to the office."

"Well, it doesn't really matter if anyone overhears us," Yuka said, "but . . . it'll be better if we can relax and talk, so why don't you come to my place?"

"Your place?"

"Yes. Oh, right—I'm registered at work as living with my parents, but actually I've got a place on my own not far from here."

"Oh, I see. Well, let's go there, then."

Yuka glanced around the street as they left the office. Having made sure that the man wasn't there, she gave a small sigh and murmured, "I feel safe when I'm with you, Sanae."

Sanae nodded, and the two of them set off to the JR station some distance away.

* * *

Sanae proceeded slowly in her utterly altered world.

She saw large white waves spreading out before her into the distance. The waves were hard and connected at the base, standing completely still, as if time had stopped. Square protrusions formed individual cocoons, and she could see organs squirming inside them. This alone was proof that this world was alive. What she'd thought of as a city until not long ago was also one large creature.

If she could never go back to the other world, it wouldn't be a problem. Far from it, everything seemed to be going much better than before.

Spellbound by the somehow nostalgic landscape of this parallel world, Sanae heard a low murmur beside her.

"Sanae, I feel you're even more affectionate than usual today."

"You do? I guess you're right . . . I feel so serene."

"I'm so glad I decided to consult you, Sanae. I feel so relaxed just being with you."

Hearing this, Sanae shifted her gaze to Yuka. The human being Yuka was no longer there. She was now a small stomach moving over the waves. And that, too, was her correct form.

The stomach moving over the surface of the creature eventually stopped before a small cocoon.

"This is my apartment. It's run-down, but still."

"It's wonderful."

As if knowing this was where it belonged, the stomach was sucked into the white cocoon. Sanae stood watching, entranced at the sight.

"Come on in, Sanae," a voice came from within the cocoon.

Coming to a halt inside, the stomach started talking in a hoarse voice.

"About my ex-boyfriend—it's not just that he's persistent, he's abnormal. He himself says that he's being weird, but he still doesn't stop. And I'm sick to death of all the emails and him lying in wait for me . . ."

As Sanae tenderly watched the trembling stomach, little by little gastric juice began to ooze from it, and drops began to flow over its surface.

"When I'm with you, Sanae, I really do feel safe and relaxed . . . I've been so scared all this time, worrying about it all . . ."

"I'm always looking out for you. After all—"

After all, you're my stomach, she'd been about to say, but then stopped. She'd felt a vibration outside.

"Sanae . . . I feel you're somehow wrapped around me."

"You do? You can cling to me as much as you like, you know."

"Thank you—really, I mean it . . . Oh! I've just been talking about myself without even offering you some tea or anything. I'm so sorry! Which do you prefer, tea or coffee?"

"Either is fine."

"Well then, I'll make some tea. Please wait a moment."

As Sanae watched the stomach moving around the small cocoon, she stroked her own pale surface. The heart that had been within her until yesterday must have slipped out without her noticing, and now it seemed there was nothing inside.

Just then, she again felt something feverish vibrating outside.

She knew it was her own heart arriving.

"Welcome home," she murmured, sticking her face outside the cocoon. The heart had been excreted, but had now come back. She had the feeling that she'd been waiting for this day for a long time.

Sanae could hear the heart beating quietly outside, along with the sound of air being sucked in. The moment it saw Sanae, it began trembling. She couldn't help feeling happy at how alive her own heart was, and she reached out to pull it to her.

"D-don't touch me!" the heart screamed, recoiling from her.

"What's wrong?"

"Sanae, are you okay?" she heard her stomach shout behind her. "Makoto, how many times do I have to tell you? Don't come here anymore!"

"Yuka, t-this woman is weird. She's wrong in the head!"

"*You're* the weird one!"

"E-even when I've been loitering for hours, she doesn't get suspicious and comes up to me smiling, as if it's the most normal thing to do. What the hell's wrong with her!"

Sanae couldn't understand why her heart would say something like that. True, she was probably living in a parallel world, but her world and the world in which they were not internal organs but human beings were two sides of the same coin and could coexist in perfect harmony. Like pieces of a puzzle fitting perfectly together, residents of the two worlds could surely live together.

"What the hell are you talking about, you bastard! You've been sending me hundreds of emails every single day, you lie in wait for me, and I've had enough! I'm going to report you to the police. Get out of here right now!"

"Yuka . . ."

The heart started trembling violently. A transparent liquid began oozing out of it and dripping down.

"Look at me! This is how much I love you!"

The stomach screamed, and Sanae saw that blood was flowing from the heart. So it really *was* her heart, she thought happily.

"Stop it! Stay away from me!"

"Why do you keep saying that? I can't control myself, that's all."

Sanae took a step toward her heart. "It's okay, just come to me. You'll feel so peaceful."

"Sanae, you shouldn't be so nice to this kind of guy. I'm going to call the police right now!" the stomach said in a low voice, and blood flowed even more fiercely from the heart.

"Just come to my world, okay? When you do, nobody will ever think of you as foreign matter again."

"What the fuck . . ."

"Whatever parallel worlds we're living in, as long as the pieces of the puzzle fit perfectly together, we can all live together forever."

Sanae enclosed the heart within her gray arms.

"Sanae, even a guy like this . . ." she heard the stomach murmur, as though impressed.

Sanae became engrossed in the beating of the heart that was struggling inside her. Unlike the organs that she'd felt to be somehow distant from her until now, this heart was now one with her. By coming to this world, she could finally become one with her own organ. She savored the heartbeat as she squeezed it with all her might, and in response the heart struggled even harder.

Sanae's flesh began responding to its vigorous movements, as if to prove that she and the heart were now one. Sweat welled up out of her skin, and she could feel her temperature rising. She almost laughed out loud. *Yes, we are just one creature!* Her flesh was beginning to stir with life, in sync with the heart. The sweat that oozed from Sanae now was a slimy body fluid, quite different from the water she'd had inside until now. She could tell that her own body was being activated more and more each moment. The stench of her internal organs erupted from her mouth, and sticky sweat flowed from her whole body.

She squeezed the heart even tighter, as if applauding it, and the heart beat harder in response to her voice, setting her flesh trembling.

Eating the City

As I headed to get some lunch, the automatic door to the office building opened in response to my presence, and warm humid air immediately pressed in on me. It was still early spring, but the steaming hot air that enveloped me was more reminiscent of summer, and memories of childhood vacations suddenly rose up in the back of my mind. It was always the same when I detected the scents of summer. It would be the same for anyone, their sense of smell responding to the summer scent that linked back to memories of vacations, bringing up vivid, nostalgic scenes.

Until I left elementary school, it was our family's custom for the three of us to get in the car, drive to my father's childhood home in the countryside, and stay there for a week over the Obon festival. It was a typical country house, deep in the mountains of Nagano. We would drive up a narrow mountain road to reach the house, which had an entrance hall about the same size as a child's bedroom and an atmosphere completely different from our house in Saitama. I was so fascinated by the old house that as soon as we arrived, I would immediately start running around and exploring, but with all the rooms connected by sliding paper doors, I would soon get lost and then burst in on the room where the adults were relaxing. They would scold me, but as soon as they let me go, I would be off again, running around and sliding doors open. Once I finished exploring inside, I played outside to my heart's content until it was time for dinner. Then I was hungry, so would keep peeking in on the kitchen, where my mother and grandmother were cooking. I was a picky eater, but to my parents' delight, I ate twice as much as usual when we were in the mountains. The vegetables Granny brought in from her vegetable garden were much sweeter than those we ate at home. Wondering why that was, I'd open my mouth wide and bite into vegetables that I never normally ate.

Absorbed in such universal memories of summer vacation, I went into the café next to the office. When my order arrived, I immediately opened the large sandwich, picked out the slices of tomato, and flipped them onto the plate. My colleague Yuki was eating raw tuna with avocado on a bed of rice, and laughing, she tucked her dyed-brown permed hair behind her ears.

"You're doing it again, Rina. Why don't you just ask them to leave it out from the start?"

"I did, but it was in there anyway."

The menu at this place was popular for its fusion of Western and Japanese rice dishes and well-stuffed sandwiches, and the café was always crowded with women office workers. And it was true—the thick, freshly BBQ-grilled hamburgers were delicious, but I couldn't help grimacing at the unappetizing smell of the vegetables stuck to the bread.

Normally we ate our lunch at work, Yuki with her homemade bento and me with a sandwich or rice ball from the convenience store. Today was payday, though, so we had decided to treat ourselves. I was fussy about food and didn't really like going out to eat. When I was with work superiors, even now, at the age of twenty-six, I couldn't bring myself to say I didn't like certain foods and usually forced myself to swallow everything, but Yuki and I were the same age, and we got along well and often went out together, so I didn't have any qualms about also removing the disgusting bit of lettuce and leaving it on the side of the plate.

"Not eating vegetables is bad for you, you know."

"Yeah, I know. I used to eat them more when I was a kid."

"That's funny. Usually you grow out of not liking vegetables!"

The reason I grew even fussier about food when I left my parents' home in Saitama and started living alone in Tokyo was not that I didn't like vegetables, but because the vegetables in Tokyo were horrible. I did sometimes leave vegetables on the plate at home, too, but the tomatoes and eggplants and other vegetables we were sent from the countryside, and the food from the nearby honesty stall, where they sold cucumbers and things, was always delicious. *You have got a pampered tongue, haven't you?* Mom would often say, laughing at me, but they were completely different foods to me. Our local supermarket had a lot of precooked dishes and bentos, but there was only a small selection of fresh vegetables and wilted meager leaves sold in single portions. With this thought in mind, I bit into my sandwich and immediately noticed the unpleasant taste of the green juice from the tomato slices that had soaked into the bread. I grimaced and washed it down with cold water.

"I think I can eat fresh vegetables, though."

"So why don't you make a small vegetable patch on your balcony?" Yuki asked.

I shook my head. "That's not going to work—I've killed at least three cactuses. And I don't have the space for it anyway."

"Oh, there's a place near me that delivers pesticide-free vegetables direct from the farm. That would be okay, wouldn't it? But they're expensive, I guess."

"That's the problem. The tasty vegetables are all expensive, and the cheap ones taste awful. They have this unpleasantly weird kind of taste, don't you think?"

"It doesn't really bother me, to be honest."

After the meal, I swallowed an array of supplements, knowing full well that it would be better to eat a proper meal. The bits of squashed tomatoes were piled up on the plate, discharging their sticky green innards into the scattered bread crumbs.

That evening, when I left work, the air was considerably colder than at midday. I took a shawl out of my bag and put it over my shoulders, glancing at my watch. Half past five. It was about the time we got busy in the kitchen when we were in the mountains in the summer, I thought nostalgically, for no reason at all.

Now that my grandmother was dead, nobody was living in the house, and there was even talk of demolishing it. Back then, though, the house in the mountains was especially lively during the Obon festival, and preparing meals for everyone was a lot of work. While all the women relatives, Mom and Granny included, prepared a huge amount of food, the children usually took a nap, tired out from playing. I would often watch TV, bored as my younger cousins were sleeping, and then Dad would take me out for a walk. We would go past the watermelon chilling in a narrow stream of water from a faucet and the old disused well, then out of the garden onto the mountain path. "Did you know that you can eat these, Rina?" he would ask, plucking a little food from the mountain—wild strawberries, maybe, or some small leaves. On either side of the path, pale and dark green undergrowth grew tangled together, with black thickets farther in. I was scared of big insects jumping out at me from all directions, and I shrank back, but Dad thrust his hand into the greenery with a practiced air and then passed me a piece of the mountain. As I bit into it, warm juice oozed out.

One day Dad picked up a stick in the garden. It was Y-shaped, thick and sturdy. "Oh, this is perfect," he said, stroking it with a nostalgic look on his face. "You put a rubber band here and use it to shoot small stones. I used to do it all the time."

I quickly took the rubber band from my ponytail and held it out to him. "Show me! Please?"

"It won't work with that one," he said, laughing. "But okay, I'll try." He went back inside the house to get a large, chunky rubber band and a small, thick scrap of cloth.

"What's that bit of cloth for?"

"What? Oh, that's where you put the stone."

He sat on the veranda and took a gimlet out of the toolbox to make a couple of holes in the cloth; then he threaded the rubber band through them. He stretched and loosened the rubber band a few times, holding on to the cloth, then abruptly stood up and said, "Okay, Rina, let's go." He seemed strangely excited as he strode off quickly, leaving me to scamper after him.

When we reached the mountain path, he said, "Don't make any noise as you walk," and he gazed at the sky as if searching for something. Eventually he stopped and whispered in my ear, "There's one! Be quiet and wait here for me, Rina, okay?"

He picked up a few pebbles from the path and left me there, crouching over as he went deeper into the grass. I held my breath as I watched him approach a large tree and put a stone in the cloth, then pull the band back like drawing a bow and arrow. Dad stretched the rubber band back as long as his arm, and I was about to warn him, terrified, that it might break at any moment, when he suddenly let go and the stone flew like a bullet into the branches. Birds flew up out of the tree all at once, and I was captivated by the sight. "How about that?" Dad said. "I haven't lost my touch at all!" He walked calmly over to the base of the tree and picked something out of the grass, cradling it in his hands, so I couldn't see very well what it was. Holding the object in one hand, with his free hand he held mine and started walking. I tried to see what he was carrying, but Dad's body blocked my view.

"Grill this for Rina, will you?" he said when we got to the kitchen.

"A sparrow? Whatever next! Where on earth did you find that?"

My grandmother's wrinkled face creased even more as she stood up, supporting her hunched back with one hand. She had a basket at her feet that contained the vast quantity of vegetables she had just picked for dinner.

"Come on, you help too!" Dad told me, so I sat between an aunt and an older cousin and started peeling some potatoes, but the work didn't go very quickly as I couldn't stop glancing over at what my grandmother was doing.

After a while my grandmother put something black on a piece of newspaper and handed it to me. "Watch out, it's hot."

"Give it a try, Rina," Dad said.

Nervously I stretched out a hand and took it. It looked more like a miniature mummy than a sparrow. As my grandmother watched, I bit into the charred meat. An appetizing fragrance burst out, and, being hungry, I opened my mouth wide for another bite, only to sink my teeth into bone.

My grandmother laughed. "It's all bones, not much to eat!"

"Yeah, that's true. But it's tasty, isn't it, Rina?" Dad said.

"Yes!" I nodded enthusiastically. I thought little birds ripened on trees like fruit did. Compared with the meat sold in packs, the meat you picked in the mountains was small and had a weird shape, but somehow the meat of a freshly picked sparrow still had a hint of life in it, with lots of flavors packed into the tiny body. I said the head was especially soft and tasty, and he laughed. "That's the brain. It's considered a delicacy that goes well with sake, so maybe you'll be a drinker when you grow up!"

*   *   *

Wouldn't it be nice if I could take evening walks and pick my own food, the way my father did in the mountains back then, I thought as I made my way home. There weren't many trees in the streets around my office in Nihonbashi, and this made me long even more for the scenery in my memory. There were some flower beds, but these contained well-tended flowers, with signs giving their names, and they looked more like they were on display than just growing there. Today I'd felt like taking a different entrance into the subway station and was walking along the road when I saw a large, dirty plant pot that looked as if it had been forgotten there, alone among the flower beds. Thinking that a gardener would probably dispose of it before long, I went over to it and saw a small withered tree around which thick weeds were growing, almost bursting the pot. I noticed a somewhat early flowering dandelion and reached out for it. I hadn't seen one of those for ages, I thought as I plucked the yellow flower. Seeing the hollow stem almost instantly brought back memories of playing with dandelions when I was little. I used to make toy waterwheels out of a stem and bamboo skewers, but now I couldn't quite remember how I'd done it. Looking closely at the flower, I started walking again, and an elegant elderly lady coming from the opposite direction smiled as she passed me.

Realizing that picking a dandelion must have struck her as something a little girl would do, I suddenly felt embarrassed and shoved it into my bag as I quickened my pace and headed for the station.

When I got home and opened my bag, I saw the yellow flower, looking a bit crumpled. I'd completely forgotten about it after shoving it in there, and I hurriedly took it out. I filled an empty jam jar with water and put the dandelion in it. It must have sucked up some water through its stem, for it seemed to perk up a little.

The next day, Yuki and I had lunch as usual in an empty meeting room at work. I casually mentioned what I'd done the day before, and when I came to the part about my memories of dandelions and the house in the mountains, to my surprise she leaned forward eagerly.

"How I envy you that! I've always lived in Tokyo, and my granny and grandpa are both from here too, so I've never spent time in the countryside, and I don't think I've ever played at picking flowers. And I've certainly never made a flower crown or a dandelion waterwheel. I just adore stories like this."

"Really?"

"Really! It sounds so wholesome, the kind of thing people should be doing. I mean, I go to the gym once a week, but I don't ever feel like I'm getting healthy. Going for a walk and picking flowers to decorate your room feels more luxurious than any aroma oil."

"In the real countryside, I never picked flowers or anything like that. Although my Dad used to pick wild strawberries."

"Wow, I love that even more!"

"I don't know, though. I mean, they're so laid-back there, and totally fine about doing things that are horrifying for city folks. Like, for example, when my Dad was little, he had a chicken, and he was really fond of it. But once it stopped laying eggs, my grandpa killed it and they ate it for dinner. Even Dad didn't feel particularly sorry for it, and he ate some too, saying how delicious it was."

Yuki laughed. "What's wrong with that? That's a natural process, after all. In the countryside you learn to appreciate life, don't you?"

This had gradually been dawning on me as we talked. "I've heard that mugwort grows in Tokyo too, in parks and places like that," I murmured as I munched on a convenience store bun. "Maybe I'll try picking some. Homemade mugwort mochi is completely different from the ones you buy, you know."

I'd been half joking, but Yuki nodded seriously. "Try it! Getting some exercise and picking vegetables must be doubly good for your health, right?"

I looked at my lunch. A big sweet bun and a sandwich. I hadn't had any vegetables at all this week. I was conscious of the high-calorific content of this food, too. I didn't feel like eating the limp vegetables from the convenience store or the supermarket, but I could imagine myself eating mugwort that I'd picked myself.

"Yeah, maybe I will. Maybe it would help me get over my dislike of vegetables a bit."

"If you make some mugwort mochi, let me try them, okay?" Yuki said, laughing.

"Of course," I said. Now I really wanted to eat some homemade mugwort mochi and recalled the nostalgic taste as I stuffed the last of the dry sandwich into my mouth.

The next day after work, I was in the locker room getting changed when Yuki came in a little late and looked a bit surprised at my outfit.

"Hi, Rina. Oh, you're dressed lightly today."

"Oh, hi, Yuki."

"I don't suppose you're going out looking for mugwort today?"

"Yep, and getting some exercise while I'm at it."

"I see—if you do find some, be sure to let me have a taste!"

I waved goodbye and left the locker room, straightened my back, and started walking. I had a plastic bag from the convenience store ready in my pocket. When I was still at my parents' home in Saitama, we sometimes went to pick fern and bracken shoots on vacant lots in early spring. There probably wouldn't be any fern shoots, but I'd be happy with some mugwort. And even if I couldn't find that, I was bound to find some dandelions. I knew they were edible, but hadn't ever eaten them, and they didn't look so appetizing, so I wasn't thinking of actually having any for dinner that night, but I wouldn't mind a little taste. I wasn't exactly serious about it, I just thought I'd have a bit of fun while getting some exercise.

First I went to where I'd found the dandelion the day before, but I couldn't find any others there. I picked the remaining leaves and peered into the flower beds, which were thick with weeds, to see whether there was anything worth picking, but I didn't know what any of the weeds were, so I decided to leave them.

As I put the dandelion leaves into the plastic bag, I noticed an office lady around my age eyeing me curiously. I quickly walked away, thinking that if anyone from work saw me doing this, it would be a bit difficult to explain. Just then a truck belching exhaust fumes drove past. I looked at the gray smoke spreading over the sidewalk and quickly opened the bag, took out the dandelion leaves, and threw them into the trash can at a convenience store I happened to be passing. Of course you couldn't eat plants growing by the side of a busy road. I'd been stupid for assuming unthinkingly that any dandelion would do, and I set off again in search of some clean dandelions.

I looked around in several parks. In one large park there were some shacks that looked as though they were occupied by homeless people, and when I thought of people living and relieving themselves in this park, I didn't feel like touching the earth, let alone eating anything from it. In a small children's playground, apparently where office workers came for a break, there were cigarette butts and empty coffee cans lying around. Naturally I couldn't eat anything that had come into contact with garbage, so I walked a bit farther and finally came to a park where there wasn't much trash, only to see signs saying TAKE YOUR DOG POOP HOME!" suggesting that it was popular with dog walkers. Looking for edible wild plants in the city was ill-advised after all, I thought, but I couldn't quite let the idea go, so I set off again, determined to find just one clean dandelion. I needed to find a park where there weren't any homeless people and that wasn't popular with dog walkers. I wandered around several children's playgrounds before realizing that I had come as far as Tokyo Station, so I decided to have a look in the Fountain Park.

It had been marked in green on the street map, so it came as a surprise to find that it was actually a concrete park with a number of large fountains and no greenery in sight. Somewhat disappointed, I looked around and saw that the concrete was enclosed by some raised beds that had exposed earth in them. They looked well-tended, without many weeds, although there were a few growing up around the plants. I wandered around, crouching over to see whether I could spot any dandelions. It occurred to me that I probably looked weird looking in the flower beds without even glancing at the fountains, and I quickly took a look around, but I saw only a few foreign tourists taking pictures. Tourists might think I was weird, but they probably wouldn't go so far as to complain, I thought, so I went back to hunting among the weeds, my face even closer than before.

This was a long way from the scenes in my head of picking mugwort on the empty lots near my family home and gathering chestnuts from the nearby prefectural park. I was more like a scavenging crow. Far from feeling enriched, I cut a pitiful figure, and worried about people seeing me, I wiped the sweat from my forehead and decided to finish up quickly and go home.

I'd gone halfway around the edge of the park when I finally spotted a group of dandelions. I looked around again and, to avoid getting dirt under my nails, took out another small plastic bag that still contained crumbs from my lunch. I thrust my hand inside it and grabbed a fistful of flowers and leaves. Still with my hand wrapped in the bag, I plucked all the dandelions within reach and put them into the convenience store bag. Feeling like a pickpocket, I quickly stuffed it into my purse and started walking to the subway station. It was getting dark, and I could no longer see any people in the park. I had worn light clothing, thinking it was spring, but the night air was unexpectedly chilly and my shoulders felt cold.

I hurriedly threw my shawl around me and got onto a subway train, but my shoulders and hands still didn't warm up. When I got back home, I switched on the heating and put the bag on the low dining table.

I made some tea and sat at the table sipping it, staring at the bag as I warmed up. The green leaves stuck to the inside looked transparent and a bit limp, not at all like anything edible. I thought about throwing them away, but having come this far, I thought I might as well do something with them, so I took them out of the bag.

The flowers didn't look edible, so I chucked them into the wastebasket in the sink. The leaves were completely wilted: even a convenience store salad looked fresher than they did. Washing them carefully, I was about to put them back on the chopping board, but then had second thoughts, and I spread the plastic bag out on the chopping board and laid the leaves on it.

I'd had the image of eating dandelion leaves as tempura, but I had only an electric stove that didn't get hot enough for frying, and I didn't feel like going to all that trouble anyway. The leaves looked bitter, so I decided to put them in miso soup to make them more palatable. I was uneasy about not cooking them enough, so I decided to boil them first, then add the miso.

As I started cutting them up with a kitchen knife, a dark green liquid seeped out. The smell they gave off was not the sort of smell you get when cooking, more like the weeds I'd been made to pull up in the yard at school. I was overcome with the sensation of playing in the mud, not cooking. I doubted whether I would actually be able to eat them.

Anyway, I put the leaves into the pan of boiling water. I felt a bit like a witch making a potion. The color rapidly seeped out into the hot water, turning it into something that looked like fabric dye. It was a bit scary, so I threw away the colored water and added fresh water several times, cooking the leaves carefully, and by the time I finally decided to add the miso, they were utterly frazzled. As I stuck the spoon into the miso, I hesitated, feeling like I was throwing precious miso into the trash. Telling myself it would be more wasteful to put only a little in and end up making a weak, unpalatable soup, I took out a big scoop and dissolved it in the pan.

When it was more or less done and I put some in a bowl, it could have passed for miso soup with spinach. But it also looked like sewage water with trash floating in it.

I served myself some rice from the rice cooker, which had been left on all day, and put it on the table next to the soup. I felt like a kid playing house, and I had absolutely no appetite. To start with, I ate only the rice, but then I summoned my courage and took a sip of the soup.

The moment I put a lump of green in my mouth, the sight of the gray concrete fountain park I'd been in earlier came back to me. I almost spat it out at the thought that what I was eating was part of that park.

The overboiled greens had no taste and felt like bits of wet tissue paper stuck to my tongue. I had a vision of the people who had been walking around the park, and then I had the urge to vomit and quickly spat it out into a tissue. It was trash after all, I thought, seeing the wilted dandelion leaf in the middle of the white tissue paper. I threw the contents of the pan into the sink and took a pack of natto out of the refrigerator. I couldn't quite bring myself to eat that either and ended up leaving half. I brushed my teeth meticulously and gargled repeatedly, but I couldn't get rid of the sensation of that tasteless leaf on the surface of my tongue.

The next day, Friday, I started to feel unwell at work and ended up having to lie down in the tea room. Yuki brought a thermometer from the admin department and took my temperature. It was 38.5C. My normal temperature was on the low side, so just seeing those figures made me feel dizzy.

"Surely it's not because you ate some mugwort, is it? Do you have a stomachache?"

"No. Don't worry, I didn't eat any . . . actually I didn't find any after all. Seems I just caught a cold walking around in the chilly weather."

I fudged my answer, not wanting anyone to know about the pathetic figure I'd cut yesterday.

Yuki looked contrite. "Oh, no. I feel partially responsible for having put strange ideas into your head. I wish I hadn't said anything. Have you told the boss yet?"

"Yes. He told me not to overdo things and that I could go home."

"Well then, leave everything to me. Take care of yourself, and have a good rest, okay?"

I thanked Yuki for being so thoughtful, went to tell my boss that I was going home early, and left the office on shaky legs. I was sitting on the train, my head bowed, feeling awful, when I noticed that an ant was clinging to the hem of my coat. I'd been wandering around in a daze, so maybe the hem had brushed against a planter or something. I brushed the ant off with my fingertip, then closed my eyes and tried to sleep.

Somehow I managed to make it home. I took some medicine and went straight to bed, but I couldn't shake off the chills. I felt so stupid for having gone to so much trouble in the cold to pick some junk that ended up being disgusting to eat, and then catching a cold in the process. I didn't even have the energy to make some rice gruel, and I had no appetite anyway, so did my best to sleep in order to be better by Monday.

Lying there in the dim room, I began to have the sensation that I was floating. My apartment was on the first floor, so the sounds of the street rang out in the room, and every car that went by brought me back to my senses. Hearing the sounds of engines and people talking, I thought back to the house in the mountains from my childhood summers.

When you were in that house, you could hear the rustling of the trees and the chirring of insects, which made you feel the overwhelming power of the outside world. You were living amidst the presence of various other creatures. The sensation of living quietly in that little gap was pleasant, breathing air that that was blended with the breaths of countless other creatures. As a child, I too had exhaled the carbon dioxide warmed by my insides, quietly suffusing the air with my own presence.

After dark, in order to alleviate the heat a little, we would open all the windows, but even though the windows were screened, we had to make sure the place was pitch-dark before opening them, or little bugs would manage to get in somewhere. We would feel the outside world, with the faint sounds of living creatures moving around and the air that had been set trembling by the movement of the trees, pressing in on us.

After my grandfather died, my grandmother came just once to visit us in Saitama. We put her in the car and set off for Tokyo to do some sightseeing. My mother and I gazed out the windows, happy to see the night views of Tokyo for the first time in ages. My grandmother was watching us, her eyes crinkling in amusement. "It's quite different from the mountains, isn't it?" my father said, to which she responded, "It's no different at all. Here they just waste too much electricity, otherwise it's much the same," and laughed.

I thought at the time that my grandmother's take on things was far more sensible than mine, and I'd wanted to be like her. Roads probably all looked the same to her whether they were made of gravel or concrete.

I pushed back the duvet, my arms covered in sweat, and opened my eyes a crack. In the dim light I saw an ant crawl out from under my coat, where I'd dropped it on the floor. I thought I'd flicked it off in the train, but it must have clung to the inside of the hem. Normally I'd have been repelled by it and would have either thrown it outside or squashed it, but I remembered being fine with the much bigger ants that had often been crawling around the house in the mountains, so I decided to just watch it. It must have been years since I tried living with nonhuman creatures I found in my home instead of immediately getting rid of them. In the mountains, everyone calmly carried on eating, even with grasshoppers jumping around on the dining table. We had the sense of living together with creatures of various sizes. When my grandmother came to Tokyo, she might have been perfectly aware of the presence of poor-looking insects crawling around on the asphalt and the feeble rustling of the trees on the streets, which we usually didn't notice, diluted as they were by the artificial noises.

I could hear the voices of some people outside, but they were speaking in a foreign language, so I didn't understand what they were saying. As I listened, their voices began to resemble the calls of animals. In my mind they overlapped with the night presences I had sensed on the other side of the torn window screens during those childhood summers, and before I knew it, I had fallen asleep.

I slept pretty much constantly for more than two days, and when I finally woke up and looked at the bedside clock, it was five in the morning. I pushed away the damp duvet and got up. My fever had gone down, and it looked as though I would be able to go back to work today.

During this time I'd ingested only liquids and a small amount of jelly and hadn't eaten any proper food. Now that my appetite had returned, I checked the refrigerator. All that was in it was some frozen rice, so I decided to go to the convenience store and changed out of my sweaty pajamas into a sweatshirt and pants. Just then I felt something tickle my little toe, and I looked down to see the little ant climbing onto it. When I realized that it had been hanging out in my apartment all this time, I didn't feel like killing it, so I went to the front door with it still on my toe, crouched down, and gently pushed it off. Maybe it instinctively knew where the outdoors was, since it made a beeline for the door and started running back and forth beside it. I opened the door for it, and feeling a little concerned about where it would go, I put on some sandals and went outside too.

The ant moved quickly over the concrete. As a memory came back to me of the way I followed ants like this when I was little, the ant entered the roughly half-meter gap between my apartment and the fence.

Weeds grew thickly here, mixed in with cigarette butts and empty cans perhaps thrown from an upstairs window. I tried to find the ant among the weeds, but it had already disappeared. Instead, I saw two dandelions with wide, spreading leaves squeezing their way up through the tall weeds. The nearest flower was quite big and surrounded by some twenty overlapping leaves almost twenty centimeters long. I crouched down and touched the leaves, feeling how fresh they were, plump with moisture. Suddenly I was overcome by a raging hunger.

I knelt down and grabbed the base of the closest dandelion, intending to pull it out by the root. I pulled with all my strength but was met with unexpectedly strong resistance, as if in a tug of war with the ground, but as I pulled harder, the stem tore away unsatisfyingly quickly. I saw a thick, pure white forked root peeping out of a gap in the soil and realized that the plant was growing quite deep.

I stuffed the torn leaves into the pocket of my sweatpants and crouched down even more, pushing my upper body into the gap to reach the other dandelion. It wasn't as big as the first one, but it was still quite large and the ground had a firm grip on it. This time I carefully dug away the surrounding soil with my hands and pulled at it, taking care not to be too rough so that it wouldn't break in half. After a while, the surrounding earth cracked and mounded, and the root slipped out, flailing like a fish. This root was more than twenty centimeters long. It looked like a burdock root, and the smell of fresh soil rose up from the hole it left. Even so, when I peered into the hole, it looked as though there was still some root left in the soil. A small bug crawled out of the scattered earth and wandered around. Holding the dandelion with the root dangling down, I went back into my apartment and immediately began to wash it. Together with the other dandelion in my pocket, the leaves and flowers half filled a colander. Suddenly I noticed the leaves I'd left on the sink earlier, and since only five days had gone by, I threw them in too.

My hunger was so fierce I could hardly bear it. I cut the leaves and stem with a kitchen knife and threw them into a pan of boiling water, flowers and all. Little by little the water turned green and a smell rose up similar to cooking beans. Unable to wait any longer, I picked out a piece with cooking chopsticks and bit into it. As I broke the stem with my teeth, a faint green flavor somewhere between mustard spinach and rapeseed shoots spread in my mouth, along with a slight bitterness.

Having expected a strong flavor, I felt a little let down by the taste. It was really plain. While slightly bitter, it was fragrant, and rather easy on the palate. I drained the leaves and put them on a plate. Having gone to the trouble of pulling out the root, I should eat that too, I thought. It seemed similar to burdock root, so it should be good stir-fried. I quickly cut it into julienne strips and fried it in a generous amount of oil. I put it on a separate plate, then set it down next to the plate of leaves on the table.

The leaves had shrunk quite a lot from boiling and produced a rather small portion, but when I placed the dishes next to a bowl of defrosted rice, it made for a far more splendid meal than my regular breakfast. The stir-fried root had taken on an appetizing aroma, and though it was slightly bitter, the flavor was less marked than burdock root. The flowers didn't have much taste but were soft and easy to eat, and I hardly used any of the soy sauce I'd put out in case. I could hear the voices of some people standing on the street outside my window. They were speaking in Japanese, and I should have been able to understand them, but I was utterly absorbed in enjoying the green flavor and couldn't catch a word. A shrill voice blended with a low one, and they no longer sounded like language as they melted down into a simple vibration in the throats of animals, setting the window quietly trembling.

By Wednesday I was completely over my cold and had just stood up to go to lunch with Yuki when she noticed me holding my bento and her eyes widened.

"Oh, that's not from the convenience store! Did you make it?"

"Yep."

As always, we staked our places in the empty meeting room and sat down. Yuki peered curiously at my lunch and pointed at some fried greens covered in plastic wrap.

"I don't suppose you picked that yourself somewhere?"

"I did. I couldn't find any mugwort, but there were loads of dandelions."

"Dandelions? Are they edible?"

"Of course. They're often used in tempura and things, aren't they?"

"I don't know, but . . . better not to risk it. They're just weeds, right?"

I raised my head and looked at her. She seemed troubled, as though seeing a child picking something up off the floor and eating it. I remembered that I'd felt the same way until now, and I smiled at her.

"Oh . . . maybe you're right," I said. "Okay, I won't." I wrapped the dandelion stir-fry up again, thinking I'd eat it at home later.

"What about this?" she asked, pointing at the omelet that contained obako leaves.

If I couldn't eat that, I wouldn't have anything but rice left for lunch, so I quickly told a white lie. "My grandmother in the countryside sent me that."

Yuki looked relieved and laughed. "Really? Wow, does she grow it?"

"No. She probably picked it on the mountainside."

"Oh, how wonderful! Of course, you can't do that in the city."

"Right."

While giving token responses to her questions, I tasted the omelet. The obako leaves mixed in with the egg had a robust vegetable flavor. I'd been researching the topic and had discovered that dandelions were originally imported as vegetables and were sold in grocery stores abroad. Yuki obviously hadn't known that when she reacted so strongly against them, while feeling that weeds picked in the mountains were fine. I watched her somewhat scornfully as I ate my lunch. If you had the intention to live a decent life, you could do so anywhere. I felt a bit stupid myself for not having realized this before, simply because I'd always lived in the city.

I started eating wild vegetables every day. The best time to look for weeds was in the evening, when I was feeling hungry. That day too, after work, I changed into some lightweight clothing to go out to harvest my dinner. I had the feeling that this was more like true labor than the time I spent tapping away at the PC keyboard or calculator on my desk.

I wanted to walk around the office neighborhood while it was still light. It wasn't so effective to go when it was dark, as I couldn't tell plants apart and there was less of a chance to discover a new harvest location.

I looked down in satisfaction at my sneakers, which were pale blue but had already gotten dirty with soil. Until recently I had forgotten that sneakers look good when they're dirty like this. I ran my hungry gaze over the surroundings as I walked along the street among men in stifling suits and meticulously dressed women. Now that I had learned to walk like an animal, I realized how much I had been viewing the city as a collection of symbols. I had been faithfully following these artificial symbols, thinking that this turn would take me to the station, that this was a sidewalk, those places over there were restaurants, and so forth. When I ran my gaze over the world with an empty stomach, the surroundings shed the armor of these symbols and revealed their true nature. My light blue sneakers could now walk beyond those symbolic meanings, striding over the sidewalk, deeper and deeper into this new world.

I decided to have fleabane leaves for my main dish that evening, and I set off for a certain children's playground in the office district. The playground was not well cared for, perhaps even abandoned, and fleabane grew there in profusion. Just thinking about it made me feel hungry, and I naturally started walking faster. I knew exactly what was growing where in this office district, and it was my daily routine to change my route according to what I wanted to eat that day.

In addition to the fleabane in the children's playground, there were some small dandelions in the flower beds on the side of the major road nearby. There was also a small space in the back of a parking lot on that big road where a small number of obako leaves were growing among the weeds, so I was careful not to harvest too much of it at one time. Today I would eat fleabane and tomorrow shepherd's purse, I thought as I walked to the playground.

I had a sort of premonition and took an unusual turn off my route, scanning the side of the road as I went. Seeing some shepherd's purse growing profusely among the flowers in an old brick planter, I crouched down happily and picked some. My senses seemed sharper than usual today, maybe because I was hungry. The hungrier I was, the sharper my sense of smell seemed. I was totally absorbed in my newly discovered wild animal existence. Maybe something similar happened to pet cats that ended up on the streets. It was still only a small part of me, but it was certainly taking root within me.

When I got to the children's playground, I saw a homeless person sitting on a bench there. He had with him a large number of magazines that he was apparently intending to sell. I was probably more of a feral human than he was, I thought with amusement. Eating vegetables direct from the earth, taking only enough to eat today, this was a healthy way to live. You could even safely eat a small amount of clover if you cooked it, and fish mint leaves that had been boiled and rinsed in fresh water no longer smelled so strong, and surprisingly they lost their bitter flavor when cooked with miso or stir-fried in oil. I particularly liked fleabane fried with bacon, and I'd started to get withdrawal symptoms if I didn't eat it every three days or so. Dandelion root was good fried and flavored with soy sauce and sugar, and was fragrant fried with no flavorings. With such delicious fresh vegetables so close to hand, I had no desire to buy those wilted leaves in the supermarket.

As I walked to the station carrying my bag of shepherd's purse and fleabane, I ran my eyes over my surroundings, thinking that I might just harvest one more type of plant for tomorrow's breakfast.

Walking like this, feeling like a feral human, even machines and buildings were warm to the touch, and some even emitted sounds and vibrations. Their presence was similar to the sounds emitted by life-forms in the forest.

I heard a faint hum behind me and turned to see a vending machine standing on the side of the road. I went up to touch it and felt the body heat of a vending machine on my palm.

Satisfied that the low voice and vibrations coming from inside it were being transmitted through my skin, I started walking again. Two-legged animals were walking around on the sidewalk, their various cries intermingling shrill howls and low growls rising up through vibrating Adam's apples.

Since the night when I'd realized that the noises humans emitted had first been animal cries and then called language, I'd been able to listen to them purely as sounds.

Several taxis were stopped on the side of the road, the heartbeats of their engines ringing out in unison. A silver lump spewing hot breath flowed past them along the river of coagulated gray liquid. Buildings stood quietly on either side of the river, and the organs at work inside their bodies gave off waves of heat that were faintly perceptible outside. I was floating in the middle of a gray ocean, and a big silver fish approached from afar, making a sound that rent the air as it approached, ruffled my surface, and receded again.

The city was filled with the presence of various beings. The vibrations of air really were the same as the ones I'd felt those summer nights in the mountains.

Pushing my way through the hubbub of living creatures, aware of my empty stomach, I picked just enough for tonight's meal from the gaps in the city. The presence of living creatures seemed to spread far and beyond into vast space. I too became part of the commotion, setting the air trembling with my breath as I moved around, permeating the streets with living vibrations.

Suddenly I noticed a clump of clover growing alongside an artwork placed outside an office building. I'll put some of that in an omelet for breakfast tomorrow morning, I thought happily, pressing my face against the artwork as I thrust my hand into the patch of weeds and plucked some leaves.

I peered into my now rather heavy bag, and a smell of green wafted up. Satisfied, I was about to get up to leave when a sudden thought occurred to me and I ran my hand over the soil I had just dug up.

I could feel the damp and warmth coming from it. With my hand still thrust into the soil there next to the artwork, I savored the sensation of the earth that had raised my food for me. Nutrition nurtured by the earth flowed into my palm. I pushed my hand even deeper into the soil, and it overflowed the gaps in my fingers, staining my sallow hand brown. My hand looked like a tree. Normally I was different from plants, separated from the earth, but I was growing out of the earth too. Evidence of this was the fact that the plants I had picked in this city were spreading to all corners of my body. I squeezed together the fingers growing in the soil. My fingers and the soil mixed together, melded, and stared up at the plants growing out of them.

I was taking my usual route home from work, picking today's weeds and putting them in the bag as I went. I'd come to a park to pick some fish mint, and I noticed a child squatting down. I went a bit closer and saw that he was digging what looked like a grave. Next to him, a small pale blue bird lay on its side alongside a strangely elaborate Styrofoam gravestone with the bird's face and name drawn on it in colored pens, and origami flowers stuck all over it, even on the back. The boy looked solemn. Still holding a fistful of fish mint, I decided to say something to him.

"What are you doing?"

He looked up at me. "I'm making a grave," he answered, and went back to being engrossed in his work.

What would my grandmother have said to such a symbolic way of mourning the death of a bird? I wondered. Remembering what I'd told Yuki about my father and his chicken, I gently whispered to the child's back, "Why not eat it?"

"What?"

"Grilled bird is delicious, you know. I've eaten it before. It's fine to return them to the earth, but I don't think the bird will really understand having such a human-style grave. I think maybe it would make the most of the bird's life if you ate it."

I thought I was being helpful, but the boy's face crumpled and he started crying. A woman, probably his mother, started coming over to us, and I quickly stood up and ran out of the park. I glanced behind me to see the boy clinging to his mother's skirt, bawling.

I didn't know why I had to run away, but certainly the mother would have treated me as a weirdo.

Before I knew it, I had wandered into mysterious territory. I could say more definitively than ever that I was sane and more wholesome than anyone else. At the same time, a normal child was in tears, complaining to his mother that I was abnormal. I walked fast, clutching the fish mint leaves in my hand. It was natural for someone living in the forest to eat the forest, and likewise it was natural for someone living in the city to eat the city. But if I said anything of the sort to that boy, no doubt he would cry harder.

It was just that it hadn't occurred to them. If they tried it, the memories of the wild rooted in their flesh would come back to them, and they would discover that eating the city like this would connect the earth between the gaps in the concrete and their own body. They would understand how natural this was, but they just wouldn't try it. As I walked, I took a bite of the fish mint leaves clutched in my hand.

It was the first time I'd tasted this pungent plant without cooking it. The moment I placed it in my mouth, its particular smell and sour taste filled my senses. The strong flavor was reminiscent of celery, and in order to hold on to it, I stuffed some more leaves into my mouth. My inner organs were set trembling by its living taste, a taste that didn't exist in the dead bodies of the vegetables lying cold in the supermarket displays. I continued walking determinedly along the gray streets, chewing on the fragments of the city, dissolving them in saliva, swallowing them, and feeling them fall into my stomach.

*   *   *

The next day, when Yuki and I went to have lunch in the meeting room, she peered curiously into my bento box. "What a lavish-looking lunch you have today."

"Yes. I just got sent lots of vegetables from the mountains. I made some dishes this morning before they go bad. Would you like to try some?"

"Really? Well, just a little then."

"Yes, go ahead! My grandmother must have picked them in the mountains."

I knew very well how much Yuki liked hearing me talk about the mountains, so I placed sample after sample of the various dishes on top of her bento as I talked to her about the mountain landscape, the touch of the grass on your feet as you walked through it, and the huge bugs that you never saw in Tokyo.

"Delicious!"

"Really?"

My plan was to draw her into my new vision of nature here in the city while taking care not to provoke a negative response. I had to avoid prematurely shocking her, paying deliberate respect to her perception based on her current understanding of common sense. I had to gently, caressingly stimulate her empathy and slowly, slowly, pull her over to my world. I had already managed to infiltrate her mind with some feral sensations. Now I would steep her in that world more and more until she was almost drowning in it.

I now felt as though I was beginning to eat the city in a different sense than before. Once I had finished marinating Yuki, how would I get started on the next person? Utmost care had to be taken over that first caress. For example, I could start by mentioning the feeling of homesickness aroused in me upon stepping out of the gray office on a warm spring day and suddenly noticing the smell of summer in the air, the sort of comment anyone could empathize with, and gradually start blending in my own feral sensations. The story could be chanted like a magic spell. Little by little it would penetrate the target body and slowly change that person.

Yuki was eating some boiled shepherd's purse dressed with soy sauce and bonito flakes. She looked at me with a smile. "You know, Rina, whenever you talk about the mountains, I feel kind of nostalgic, even though I don't have memories of a home in the countryside myself. Strange, isn't it?"

"I guess it happens. Maybe that sort of thing is hardwired in our genes. Oh, I was going to say that Granny sometimes sends chicken meat too. Next time I'll bring a little along to share. Talking about the house in the mountains, did I ever tell you?

UntilIleftelementaryschoolitwasmyfamily'scustomfor thethreeofustogetintothecaranddrivetomyfather'schildhoo dhomeinthecountrysideandstaythereforaweekovertheObon festival,itwasatypicalcountryhousedeepinthemountainso

fNaganoandwewoulddriveupthenarrowmountainroadto
reachthehousewhichhadanentrancehallaboutthesizeofachi
ld'sbedroomandanatmospherecompletelydifferentfromour
houseinSaitama,Iwassofascinatedbytheoldhousethatassoon
aswearrivedIwouldimmediatelystartrunningaroundand
exploringbutwithalltheroomsconnectedbyslidingpaper
doorsIwouldsoongetlostandthenburstintheroomwhere
alltheadultswererelaxingandgetscoldedbutassoonastheylet
megoIwouldbeoffagainrunningaroundslidingdoorsopenan
donceI'dfinishedexploringinsidenextIwouldplayoutsideto
myheart'scontentuntilitwastimefordinnerandIfelthungry"

I continued murmuring these tender words. Little by
little the memories slipped into Yuki's body and wriggled
around in her innards. After a while, they would be flowing
unnoticed around her whole body, and she would gradually
lose her physical sense as she knew it now—just like the
marvelous change that happened to me a short while ago.
And then we would start to live a wholesome existence
together in this world teeming with life.

Hatchling

"Haruka, have you decided which friends you're inviting to the wedding?" Masashi asked.

"Oh, sorry! I got the replies to my email, but haven't got round to doing anything yet," I answered lazily.

"Oh, come on. Make sure you do answer them. They'll be going out of their way to come, so make up the list quickly. You're so untogether, I swear!"

"Yeah, I know. Sorry!"

"Well, I guess being super laid-back and doing everything at your own pace is one of the good things about you."

"Okaaaay!"

Masashi looked a little incredulous, but he didn't seem too annoyed. He was used to me being sloppy, and he was generally pretty cheerful and not too hung up on details. He'd been like that ever since we met. He was a little simple, but he had a sunny personality, and since we were both a bit messy, we got along well.

"Oh, and what are you doing about the speeches? I've asked my boss and a friend."

"Oh, right. Um, I was thinking of asking Aki to do that."

"Aki's your childhood friend, right? That sounds like a good idea," he said.

Just then my smartphone beeped on the sofa where I'd left it. I looked at the screen and saw that a message had come in from a friend from back home: "Hey, Prez, about the next lunch party—aren't we celebrating Miho's promotion? Should we prepare something special?"

Still lying on the floor, I quickly replied, "Sure, I'm on it. I've ordered flowers and one of those notebook covers she always said she liked, with her initials on it. It should be ready in time."

The reply came instantly. "Fantastic. I should have known! You haven't changed a bit since you were a kid, have you? Masashi's gonna have it easy when he marries you. You always arrange things so efficiently."

I was about to reply when another message came in. This time it was from Rika, a friend from film club in college.

"Princess, this is where we'll be having next week's celebratory drinks party."

I replied immediately. "Rika, thank yoooouuuuu ♡ ♡ ♡"

"We were all so excited when we heard you were getting married! After all, you were always our club's princess!"

"Not at all! I'm sorry you had to contact everyone yourself, though, since I'm not on social media (;o;)"

"No problem, but you should get yourself online. Everyone else is!"

"I signed up once, but didn't really get the hang of it (*>_<*)"

During this exchange with Rika, messages came in from someone I used to do a part-time job with in college days, a friend from high school, and a colleague from work. I quickly replied to all of them attentively, taking care not to mix up the addresses.

"I'm sorry, but I don't really like drinks parties. Could you possibly give them my apologies?"

"You whaaaaat? Right on!!!! Send me a pic. Let's brag about it to Okamoto!"

"I want a picture from university days. I've been look-ing for one, but can't find anything good (*;∇ ;*) I want to use it in a slide show at the wedding."

"For the lunch party, as well as the gifts, I've also arranged for a surprise cake. I'll be going early to set every-thing up, so if anyone wants to come and help, please do!"

"What, really? I had no idea! I'd better send some flowers!"

I'd been so absorbed in replying to all the messages, before I knew it Masashi had already had a shower. He came out of the bathroom drying his hair with a towel and sat down on the sofa.

"Haruka, you've still got a bunch of messages you haven't replied to, haven't you? You're hopeless, really. So untogether!"

"I guess . . ."

"You really are! I'm closer to you than anyone, and even I'm saying that!" He started blow-drying his hair.

"I guess you're right!"

I laughed foolishly, and Masashi couldn't help breaking into a smile.

Soon after I started at university, I realized that I didn't have a personality of my own.

When I was a child, I was a straight-A student. I always did what adults told me to, so I was nicknamed Prez. I was good at studying and was often charged with class rep duties, so I never doubted that it was my natural disposition.

After graduating from junior high and going on to senior high, I was the only one from my old school there. During the first class, when I took my textbook and exercise book out of my desk, a girl with dyed brown hair next to me said, "Wow, what on earth? You wrote your name on the textbook! Oh! And on your exercise book too."

I'd only followed the instructions on the printouts distributed to us all at the opening ceremony. It never occurred to me that I'd be laughed at for it, so I simply smiled.

Seeing my expression soften, the girl seemed to relax and grew a little friendlier. I noticed that our facial muscles seemed to be moving in response to each other, and I couldn't help smiling even more broadly.

"Can I see your other books?" she asked, reaching out to take them from my desk. "Wow, look at this kid! She's written her name on everything! That's hilarious!"

She held up the books on which I'd carefully written my name so all the others could see them. My expression must have been so sheepish that they interpreted it as permission to make fun of me, and they all burst out laughing.

I thought I could respond better to everyone's expectations, and before I knew it, a goofy voice came out of my mouth. "Oh, but that's what the teacher told us to do, isn't it? I thought everyone would do it!"

Everyone laughed even harder at my inane way of speaking.

"What a goofball! This one's a total basket case. So funny!"

"What? Hey, I'm not a goofball!"

Where did this way of speaking suddenly come from? I wondered. When I saw all the girls laughing, I'd suddenly started acting out the "me" they imagined me to be.

The brown-haired girl seemed to have taken a shine to me.

"You're a hoot! What's your name again?" she asked.

"Haruka . . . Takahashi . . ." responding to them in an inane voice, as if we were doing a jam session.

Before the day was out, I had turned into a girl who was a goofball and a bit dumb. The Prez of my junior high school days had gone, and before I knew it, everyone was affectionately calling me Peabrain.

"What the heck, Peabrain, you're such a goof!"

The weird thing was, even if I did exactly the same things I did when I was Prez, everyone now laughed at me, stroking my head and nudging me affectionately.

"You'll never get a boyfriend, Peabrain. You're just too goofy!"

"Whaaat? No way . . ."

The way I spoke changed after I became Peabrain. But I didn't feel all that different from when I'd been Prez. It wasn't really me speaking, I was simply reacting automatically in the way everyone seemed to want me to.

I gradually got used to being Peabrain. Peabrain only ever said inane things and was loved by all her classmates.

Finally it was time to take the entrance exam for university, and I ended up going to a university where nobody else from my high school was going.

All my friends said things like "Peabrain, will you be okay without us?" and "We worry about you. You're such a goofy Peabrain, after all."

Everyone told me I should join a club at university to make friends, so I followed their advice and joined the Film Appreciation Club. All we did was watch movies, eat, drink, and make booklets of our reactions to the films. Even Peabrain me could do that much, I thought.

"Hello, everyone! I'm Haruka Takahashi! Are you a fresher too?" I asked one guy who was obviously older, trying to flatter him. *Me, a newbie? Don't be silly!* he would say, slapping me on the head, and everyone would laugh. It would be a perfect Peabrain move.

"No, of course not!"

"Are you nuts?"

Just as I'd expected, the laughter spread. It looked like I'd easily be able to pass as Peabrain here, too. Just then a commanding voice rang out.

"How utterly adorable! I just love airheads like her!"

It was a strikingly beautiful older student called Reina. Since she made this declaration, other girls started whispering, "It's true, she is an airhead" and "So cute!" In a flash, a completely different response from the Peabrain one spread like a chemical reaction.

"And I adore pretty girls like you, Reina!" I said, assessing the atmosphere of the place in an instant and giving Reina a hug.

"There, there," Reina said, stroking my hair.

One of the guys said teasingly, "Hey, you're just my type. Give me your address, won't you?"

I was wondering how I should react to his half-joking tone when Reina said sharply, "*Oi*, Itaya, stop trying to pick her up. You'd better watch out, Haruka, the guys in this club can't be trusted. I'll look out for you."

"Sure!" I said enthusiastically. I'd merely been adapting myself to the mood, but now everyone started spinning words in response.

"Haruka, that's not fair!"

"Have you got a boyfriend, Haruka? If not, give me a chance, won't you?"

"Let's go out on a date soon!"

Now "I" was being rapidly turned into a new character without even saying anything else.

It became normal for guys in the film club to chat me up and for Reina to beckon me over to her side: "Haruka, come over here to me, I have to get you out of danger!" The same exchange was repeated over and over whatever the occasion, whether a party, a barbecue, or a movie night.

Before I knew it, everyone in the club had started calling me Princess.

It wasn't as though my appearance had changed from when I was Peabrain, and I knew very well that the guys were actually after beautiful Reina, not me. But little by little, in response to the expectations of this new character, I started changing the way I dressed as Peabrain to outfits more suitable for Princess.

I replaced the sweatshirts with dumb cartoon characters and baggy pants that my goofy Peabrain character had worn, choosing pink or white lacy dresses appropriate for Princess. I had no sense whatsoever of what I wanted to wear, I just wore whatever was dictated by the character my surroundings had created for me.

I decided to take a part-time job at a family restaurant that had cutesy Princess-like uniforms.

"Well then, Takahashi, help all the others take these things to the storeroom, will you?"

"Okay!" I responded enthusiastically.

Clad in my uniform and pure white apron, I joined all the others who were moving a food delivery of vegetables, frozen goods, and other items, and made a beeline for the heaviest item, a barrel of beer.

This is what I always did as Princess. In the film club, whenever we held barbecues, or in other situations involving carrying things, I always took the heaviest item. Then one of the guys would always come over, saying, "I'll help you with that, Princess," and add teasingly, "So give me your email address, okay?" And one of the other girls would always say, "Stop that! You'll get into trouble with Reina if you start hitting on Princess," and then add, "Come on, Princess, come over here and help me prepare the vegetables." That was the way it always went, so I'd done the same without thinking.

"Wow, you're taking that? It's really heavy!" I heard someone say, and turned to see a guy about my age. "Are you serious? A woman can't carry that!"

I detected a faint expectation of my character in his words, so I flexed my arm muscles and lifted the barrel.

219

"You did it! Wow!"

"Not such a big deal," I told him in a manly kind of voice.

"You're so cool, Takahashi!"

"You look so girly, I wasn't expecting that!"

And once again I simply responded to them. "Oh, come on. It's easy enough!"

"Seriously? You must be a man after all," a brown-haired guy said.

"Oh, do shut up and get that box, why don't you?" I said lightly, and carried the barrel into the storeroom.

After that, everyone at work called me by a masculine version of my name, Haruo, and treated me like a tomboy figure.

Characters escalate in their community. As Haruo, I gradually became rougher, not just in the way I spoke but also in the way I behaved, and on workdays when I didn't have to go to classes, I started changing my way of dressing to a boyish style, with simple shirts and jeans, completely unlike what I wore at college.

"Haruo, you should work in the kitchen. You'll be better there—the girly uniform really doesn't suit you!"

"Shut your face!" I said. "Oh, can someone serve that table?"

"What? You're having steak and rice, in the *morning*? No way! Are you *sure* you're a woman?"

I smiled and lightly kicked him.

"Ouch! Your kicks really hurt, Haruo!" He laughed, and everyone else in the kitchen laughed too. The more I acted like a boy, the more everyone liked me.

That's when I clearly realized something: I did not have a personality of my own.

I simply spoke in a way that I would be liked within whichever community I happened to be in. I responded to wherever I was in order to adapt to it. I was just like a robot.

I was really popular in the film club and at my workplace. If I ever went back to my childhood home, then I'd be Prez again, or at a gathering of high school friends I'd be Peabrain. However many more characters I developed, the four me's currently inside me did not contradict one another in any way. After all, I was just a machine that responded to the community in order to be liked.

Whenever I did something that was liked and praised, that part of me would develop, while if anyone said to me "That's not like you," I'd shed that part. As a result, the outline of myself was not mine at all.

But this quality was apparently not just mine. If I paid attention to other people, I often thought that a certain person was simply responding to those around them. We kept responding back and forth in our community, turned ourselves into a character, and started behaving according to that character. I began to think that maybe nobody had such a thing as a real self.

The only difference between a robot and myself was the desire to be liked or to blend in, that's all. It's not that I wanted affection, it's just that it was rational and convenient to blend into and be liked by a community. Considering that humankind had already been living in villages by the Stone Age, it was basically human instinct. If you could blend in and be well-liked by a community, you would be safe and your life would go smoothly. That was my only motive for trying to be liked.

One Sunday, Reina came to the restaurant while I was working.

"Princess! I didn't know you worked here!"

I dithered over which character's speech I should use in my reply. Eventually I managed to match myself to Reina and responded "Sure!" in a Princess tone of voice.

"The uniform really suits you! If the guys in the club get to hear about it, they'll start coming here in droves!"

"Oh, no! Please, please don't tell anyone. I'm not used to the work yet, and I'd be so embarrassed . . ."

Reina nodded understandingly. "It would be a real nuisance if the guys in the club came here in pursuit of you, wouldn't it? Don't worry, I definitely won't say anything to them. I always look after you, after all."

She ordered some coffee and a tea-flavored dessert. I went behind the counter to make the dessert, and my male coworker asked, "Haruo, who's that gorgeous girl? A friend of yours?"

"We're in the same club at college."

"Seriously? You two are completely different, aren't you? Introduce me to her, will you?"

"Give me a break. Go and clean up outside." I lightly kicked his calf like I usually did, and he went outside, laughing at this typical reaction from "Haruo."

I suddenly remembered Reina and looked over at her. She wasn't looking at me. I breathed a sigh of relief and took her coffee and dessert over to her table.

"Thank you," she said without looking at me.

When she went to pay her bill and I went behind the till, she said, "Princess, you're so two-faced."

I didn't understand what she meant and stood there vacantly with her change in my hand. She snatched the coins from my palm and left.

After that, Reina ignored me whenever I went to the film club.

Another first-year girl in the club told me that she was telling everyone behind my back that I was two-faced.

The girls in the club reassured me, saying, "She's just jealous of you, Princess. Before you came along, she was the Madonna of the club, and now she can't stand how everyone says you're cute." I knew that wasn't true, though.

I had a different character for each community I belonged to. Reina felt that this was sneaky of me, and that I was faking versions of myself.

Perhaps I was the only one who changed my character in this way. Seeing Reina being so cold to me, I suddenly felt ashamed. She hardly ever came to the club anymore, and I was left holding the masks of my split characters.

When I left college and got a proper job, I decided to do my best not to respond to my environment so much.

The company I started working for rented out scaffolding for construction sites. It was a homely work environment, and maybe because its headquarters were located in fun-loving Osaka, the employees often went out drinking together, but I didn't join them very often. I ate my lunch alone and didn't talk to anyone unless it had to do with work.

Before I knew it, everyone at work was calling me Mysterious Takahashi. When I asked why, an older female colleague smiled and, patting me on the back, said, "Well, it's because you're so cool, an enigmatic lone wolf. It's a compliment, you know."

Even when I did nothing, I was still made into a character. I simply couldn't get my head around this.

Maybe many of my coworkers were indulgent, for Mysterious Takahashi was treated positively as being cool and mysterious. Whenever my superiors said things like "Do come drinking with us next time, Mysterious Takahashi," I'd reply, "No, I have other things to do," inadvertently responding to their expectations. At work I started wearing blue light-blocking glasses with a cool silver-rimmed design, and I rapidly developed into this new character.

Once a character has been defined, it never disappears, as long as its community remains in existence. Whenever I met up with childhood friends, I was still Prez, and with high school friends I was Peabrain, and I was still Princess to college club friends, while emails from my coworkers at the part-time job I did while in college were addressed to Haruo. Now I'd become Mysterious Takahashi. My life continued with these five characters progressing alongside one another.

My boyfriend, Masashi, didn't know about this. He knew me as Peabrain, since we'd been introduced by high school classmates who said, "It's about time you found someone good, Peabrain."

We'd gotten along well. Masashi was a cheerful, pleasant young man who didn't seem to be two-faced at all. But was that really the case? Maybe, like me, he too was juggling multiple characters in his life. Maybe he was known as a gloomy, moralistic old fogy at work, or a little prince in the neighborhood where he grew up. I had never talked to Masashi about the other four me's. He'd always believed I was a slightly dumb Peabrain who was easy to get along with.

Aki's reply came in the next morning. "Okay, I'll do the speech. I guess I'll have to."

I breathed a sigh of relief. "So can I come over to yours next weekend to thank you properly and discuss everything?" I wrote.

"Prez, stop being so formal with me, will you? I'll provide cake, so don't bring anything with you, okay? Come as Peabrain, please."

"Yay!!! Thank you!!!" I replied, adding some emojis Peabrain-style.

Aki and I had been friends since elementary school. And she was the only one who knew about my five "characters."

Back when I was still in college, not long after Reina had stopped coming to the film club, my old friend Aki had also come by chance into the very same restaurant where I worked. I thought it would be the end of our friendship. She, too, would curse me for having a dual personality and being two-faced. But when she saw me talking like a guy, all she said was, "Wow, Prez, you've changed!"

Our colleges were nearby, and we came from the same neighborhood, so I started going home with her after work more and more often. Then I summoned my courage and broached the subject.

"Hey, Aki. About my work persona . . ."

"Oh, that. Yeah, I was quite taken aback. But it's hardly surprising that either of us would have changed since elementary school, is it?" she said, laughing.

"Um, but there's more," I said seriously.

"More?"

226

"That's not the only one. There are other me's too." When I was with Aki, I naturally slipped into the Prez way of speaking.

Aki seemed a bit bewildered, but then she burst out laughing. "Oh, come on, Prez, you're not exactly Jekyll and Hyde. Aren't you learning anything at college? It's just normal for people to develop various personas as they adapt to their surroundings, you know."

"But I'm probably a bit abnormal. Say what you like, but does everyone have such completely different masks as I do? Is it normal for there to be nothing behind the mask? Doesn't everyone behave as though there's a 'real me' behind their mask?"

Aki tensed at my seriousness, and for a while she seemed to be thinking.

"Listen, Prez, don't you think you're overthinking things? I get the feeling that that seriousness is part of your true nature. But I'm not an expert in psychology, so I don't really know."

"So how about checking it out? I'd like you to meet the other me's."

"Well, okay . . ."

I took her to a drinking party at the film club. The moment we walked into the izakaya, I called out, "Sorry I'm late! This is my bestest friend, Aki♡" in a voice that was completely different from my usual one, and Aki looked shocked.

"Princess, you're late! We couldn't start drinking until you got here, you know!"

"Wow, is that your friend, Princess? She's gorgeous. Hey, come sit over here!"

I squeezed Aki's arm and said, "Sure! Come on Aki, let's go over there."

I sat next to Aki and clung flirtatiously to her. She was totally bewildered.

Even I didn't know why I was doing that, but Princess's speech and behavior had become automatic within me, and I spontaneously responded according to other people's words and actions.

Afterward I rejected an offer from one of the guys to see us both home, and Aki and I got the last train back together.

"What did you think?" I asked.

"Wow, I was really amazed."

"As I thought. There's something weird about me, isn't there."

Aki leaned against the handrail in the train, deep in thought for a while. "No . . . I was taken aback, but I also kind of felt that ultimately you're just doing what humans do."

"What?" I leaned forward and grabbed her. "Do you really think so?"

"Yeah . . . I was thinking about it all the time as I watched you in the izakaya. It's pretty extreme, for sure, but if you place the highest priority on making a space feel harmonious, then humans can probably become anything. That's what I thought seeing you today, Prez."

"Oh . . ."

"Prez, you've always been the sort of kid who's careful to make the class or whatever go smoothly, haven't you? Even if you're called Princess, it doesn't feel like you're just trying to be popular and have a good time. It's like you're responding to what's right in front of you. You're a bit like Palpo."

"Palpo?"

"Don't you know what that is? There's one outside the station—one of those conversation robots you see everywhere these days. It just knows some basic greetings and responds to words, so it doesn't really feel like having a conversation, and it gets a bit boring after a while. It was popular some time ago."

"Oh, I see." I think I got the idea. "Yeah, I guess I'm like Palpo. Maybe I'm a more advanced robot from the future," I mumbled absently, light-headed from too much sangria.

Aki laughed, hugged my head, and rested it on her shoulder. "Come on, Prez, you're drunk, aren't you? Get some sleep," she said.

"Okay . . ."

"Who's talking now? Prez? Or Princess? Or Haruo?"

"I don't know . . ."

"Really? Even *you* don't know?"

"I just respond, that's all. Whoever the person I'm with thinks I am, everything else follows accordingly. I'm not the one who decides who I am . . ."

I heard Aki suck in her breath.

The train was headed for the neighborhood where Prez had grown up. It was pitch-black outside the windows. The train rocked me pleasantly as I sat with my eyes closed, traveling from the place where Princess spent her time to the place where Prez lived.

That weekend I bought some cherries and went to visit Aki in her condominium. She laughed in exasperation and said, "That's just like you, Prez. I told you not to bother!"

She put the cherries on the table next to the cake she'd prepared, then brought out some tea. "So, Haruka, what are you going to do when you get married to Masashi? You'll be bringing together all the people who know Prez and Peabrain and Princess and Haruo and Mysterious Takahashi for your wedding, right? Which of them are you going to be at the ceremony?"

"That's the thing . . ."

When I was alone with Aki, I spoke like Prez. I sighed, and she looked exasperated.

"If all you had to do was make a speech, you could probably get away with it . . . but what about when the two of you have to go around to all the tables at the reception, lighting candles? Will you be changing character at each table? It's like a horror movie!"

"That's why I wanted to make it family only. But Masashi has loads of friends, and he won't hear of having anything less than a big wedding reception and after-party."

"Well, it's already decided, so there's not much you can do about that."

"What do normal people do? You're not as bad as I am, but even you said you change character a bit, didn't you? What period of your life would you take your 'me' to your wedding?"

When Aki was little, she was considered a "mature girl," but at college everyone thought of her as "a fierce, strong-willed, scary woman," and in the company where she now worked, she was apparently a "soothing elder-sister type." Maybe everyone changed character, even if not to the extent I did. So how on earth did they act at their wedding or when posting on social media?

"Either you match the self you are with your partner or the self you are with the biggest of your communities . . . I think most people make that out to be their truest self."

I sighed. How could people unify themselves so easily?

It was the same when friends in my college club pressured me into using social media. My childhood friends, high school classmates, college club buddies, part-time job friends, and my current workplace colleagues were all looking at the same site, having tracked me down somehow, and I had no idea what to write.

I didn't even know what to choose for my profile icon. A cute and colorful macaroon icon that Princess would choose would look weird to Haruo's friends, wouldn't it? And my friends who knew me as Peabrain would be really puzzled by the deep-sea fish icon that was ideal for Mysterious Takahashi.

When I looked at everyone's pages, they were full of innocent descriptions of the type of food they cooked or the places they'd been. What character had they chosen to do this? I got cold feet and quickly deleted my account.

"From my point of view, they're the ones who are crazy," I muttered suddenly.

Aki forced a smile. "I guess everyone becomes the character they want to be on the internet. If you have some kind of ideal of the sort of person you want to be seen as, I think you can easily be drawn into it—on social media too."

"Anyway, I've decided to ask Masashi. I'm fine with fitting in with him as Peabrain for our wedding, but then someone is bound to say something. It's better to come clean with him up front rather than be called two-faced, right?"

Aki nodded, looking a bit uneasy. "Yeah, I suppose that would be ideal, but . . ."

"Masashi is simple and a good person, so I think he'll understand."

Aki smiled. "Oh, I forgot . . . I got you a wedding present. You both like wine, don't you? I settled on those sparkling wineglasses you said you wanted."

"Oh, I'm sorry to put you to all that trouble! But thank you, I'm really happy."

The one who liked sparkling wine was Peabrain. Haruo preferred beer, and Princess often drank sangria. Prez was usually organizing the parties, so she drank only oolong tea or, at most, one glass of lemon sour. Mysterious Takahashi drank shochu or whiskey on the rocks.

Even though the physical body was the same, the type of alcohol had a different effect depending on the character. I knew Aki had made her choice because I was Peabrain when I was with Masashi.

"Thank you," I said, accepting her gift.

"Actually," she said somewhat hesitantly, "I have another gift I want to give you."

"What, another one? You don't need to go that far!" I said, showing the hesitation typical of Prez.

"It's been on my mind for ages, although I couldn't bring myself to give it to you before now. It didn't cost me anything, so don't worry about that," she said with a smile.

That weekend, I was lazing around in the living room when Masashi came in.

"Oh, come on, loafing around again! If you haven't got anything to do, how about getting started on our wedding plans? Honestly, you're hopeless, you really are!" he said. "I know we don't need to get on with the actual preparations for a while yet, but we were supposed to at least try on dresses and sort out the invitations early on, weren't we?"

I made up my mind. I went to the bedroom, took a file from the bookshelf, went back to the living room, and sat down at the table.

"First, there is something I would like you to choose, Masashi."

"What's that? Did the wedding hall people say something?"

"Look, at this point in time, there are five me's in existence. I can't choose which one to be by myself. So I want you to choose which one you want."

Masashi looked as though he had no idea what I was talking about.

"After giving it some thought, I decided it was maybe easiest to explain using the wedding dress. I chose wedding dresses for each me to help you understand. This floaty dress is for Peabrain. This wedding pantsuit is definitely best suited to Haruo. For Princess, I think it has to be this girly dress with lots of lace, and for Prez this traditional dress. And I think this antique dress would be a good fit for Mysterious Takahashi. So which me do you prefer?"

Masashi had been lying on the sofa, but now he sat up, frowning. "What the hell are you talking about?"

"Which Masashi will you be at the wedding, Masashi? There isn't just one of you either, surely? I thought another approach would be for me to match myself to whichever *you* you are for the wedding. Anyway, once we've decided which *me* will be there, that will settle everything else. The design of the wedding invitation, the color of the bouquet, the type of ring, the color of the tablecloth, the shape of the cake, the gift for guests—everything. Once I know which character to be, I'll be able to visualize everything else. So I want you to decide which me I should be, Masashi. Then I can get on with everything."

"What's up with you, Haruka? Seriously, has something happened?"

Masashi didn't seem to be following, so I did what I had done with Aki and carefully explained each of my five characters from beginning to end.

"But I guess just explaining it isn't easy to understand. Maybe I should show you. They actually only exist in their various communities, but I'll make an exception for you, Masashi. 'Oi, Masashi. What happened to that beer in the fridge? You drank it, didn't you? It cost an arm and a leg, that one. You gotta be kidding me!' That was Haruo. Did that shock you? The tone of voice and way of speaking is totally different, right? 'Masashi, darling, have you got some scissors? I can't find mine, and I want to cut the tag off this super cute dress I bought . . .' That's Princess. Aki often mimics Princess, doesn't she? She seems to be the easiest one to copy. 'Masashi, did you leave the nail clippers somewhere again? They're supposed to be kept here. I told you, didn't I? We're living together, so do keep it together, okay?' That's Prez. You're a bit lazy about things sometimes, Masashi, so maybe this type would be good for you. 'I'm reading just now, so can you please refrain from talking to me?' That's Mysterious Takahashi. So which character would be the easiest to live with? Any of them is fine by me, so if you can choose one, Masashi, I'll use our wedding to unify myself into her."

Masashi had gone pale and was staring at me, so Prez explained further. "Think about it. From now on, we'll be inviting friends over to our new place more often and getting people together for barbecues, won't we? It's not just a matter of simply getting through the wedding. That means I have to unify myself. However natural it is for me to adopt the persona for each particular community, everyone else will feel uncomfortable if there is too much inconsistency in my personality. Do you understand what I'm saying?"

"No! Who are you? Haruka doesn't talk like that!"

Masashi was so worked up that Princess gently soothed him. "Come, Masashi, are you okay? Calm down, there's no need to be scared. You can relax now. Haruka is a bit extreme, but really everyone is a bit like that, aren't they? Oh, how about a nice cup of hot tea? That'll help you relax, won't it, Masashi dear?"

I rubbed his back, but he jumped and pushed my hand away.

"Just who are you? You've been deceiving me . . . all this time I've been deluded. You were never the real you all along!"

"Don't you think you're overreacting a bit?" said Mysterious Takahashi. "After all, you have that side to you too, don't you? There must be different you's when you're with your family, or at work, or with me. You yourself can't say which is the true Masashi, can you?"

Masashi stood up and fled to the corner of the room.

"Stop running away, dammit!" Haruo told him. "I'm showing you all of me now. Don't try to escape these revelations. Look, nobody else is ever gonna show you so much of themselves, right? Stop covering your ears, you chicken!"

"Shutupshutupshutup!" Masashi yelled, losing his temper. "Don't say anything else! I feel like I'm going crazy. Stay away from me. And stop talking!"

He shoved me away and shut himself up in the bedroom. All the characters tried talking to him through the door, but he showed no sign of coming out. I gave up and lay down on the sofa in the living room. I reached out a hand for the bag Peabrain had left lying around.

I hadn't wanted to use Aki's wedding gift if I could avoid it, but it turned out that I'd have to after all. I sighed and took a piece of paper out of the bag.

"Here, take this," Aki had said that day, handing me a résumé on a single sheet of paper.

"What is it?"

"It's the sixth Haruka. The one I made for you."

On it was a photo of someone else, not me, and the details of that person's life and hobbies to date were written up in detail.

"Who is this?"

"A reserve Haruka. Use her if you're in a fix."

"A reserve me?"

"Haruka, if you try to unify yourself at your wedding ceremony," Aki murmured, her expression serious, "everyone is going to want to see the real you. So far we've seen only fake Harukas, so show yourself, they'll say. But you don't have a 'self,' do you? This new Haruka is for just that sort of time. If you show them this sixth version of you, I think they'll all be satisfied."

"I see . . . even Reina from college days might have been convinced by something like this?"

"Probably. From now on, you are often going to find yourself with people from different communities. That's the sort of time you'll need it. This is my wedding gift to you. Of course, I also put my heart into choosing the wineglasses."

"Hmm . . . what sort of person is this Haruka?" I asked Aki, thinking it was written in such detail that it would be quicker to hear it than read through it.

"I made her ugly."

"Ugly?"

"People have more faith in ugliness." Aki smiled scornfully, gracefully crossing her legs. "People are more easily taken in by ugly things, not lovely things. That's reality, they'll say, that's the truth! Then they follow their own imagination and make up a banal story to satisfy themselves, and they feel reassured."

"But why?"

"Dunno . . . but when you follow beautiful words with nasty ones, pretty much everyone will crow about how you've spoken truthfully. And if you do the opposite, they'll lament that you're a hypocrite with your lies. Maybe they find it more reassuring that way. They just can't relax with the idea of truth being lovely."

"That's weird," I muttered.

Aki stroked my head. "I hope you don't have to use it, that you can keep it as a reserve self. I prepared it for you as a kind of talisman, just in case. Something to use in an emergency."

"Thank you, Aki."

I'd been happy to receive the glasses, but more than anything, I was grateful for Aki's willingness to put so much effort into understanding me to the best of her ability.

"I'll let you use my gift at home with Masashi, but how about we have a toast together now too?"

"Sure!"

And so the two of us had clinked our glasses before the résumé.

"Prez, congratulations on your wedding!"

"Thank you. I'll cherish your gift, Aki. Here's to the sixth me!"

Aki burst out laughing, and our peals of laughter rang out around the room along with the clink of our glasses.

The next morning, I awoke on the sofa to the sound of Masashi's footsteps.

"Good morning," I said.

Looking uncomfortable, he said, "Sorry to have kept the bedroom to myself," and went into the kitchen, keeping his eyes averted from me.

"Before breakfast, there's something I want to tell you," I said.

"Tell me?"

"I'm sorry that I've been deceiving you all this time. I want to confess my true self to you."

His eyes widened.

"To be honest, I'm a hideous woman. I've always loathed the world and cursed it, and I've spent my whole life covering up that self. And to tell the truth, I've always been jealous of you, Masashi. I'm like a monster, hating everything that's wholesome."

Masashi looked stunned. I continued in an even voice with my fictitious confession.

"Ever since I was little, I've lied about myself in order to be loved. Being starved of affection gradually killed the existence of my true self. Whoever I was with, I tried to gain affection by playing a fictitious character. But inside, the child me was always crying.

"Eventually I started to hate the world. I behaved in ways to make me be liked, and at the same time I began to be obsessed with fantasies of killing people who lived happily. Seeing my best friend, Aki, being accepted and loved just as she was, I was so jealous of her that I even hid her indoor shoes at school. Just because I envied her. I hated everyone who was loved and happy. Even though I knew it wasn't their fault, I couldn't control my consuming hatred.

"When I met you, Masashi, I knew you were a perfect target for me. You're so cheerful and easygoing, and everyone loves you. By getting my hands on someone like you, I'd be getting my revenge on the world. But I couldn't control my feelings of jealousy. Remember that super spicy soup I made? Hatred made me do that. And it was me who hid your ear cleaner and changed the bathroom light for an old one."

"You . . ."

"It was me who erased your recording of that soccer program too. I can't control my hatred of the world. My hands move all on their own accord."

I didn't for a moment think he would believe such trite stories. However simple and easy to deal with he was, surely nobody would accept falsehoods like this. Despite my doubts, though, I went down on my knees to him. I pressed my palms together as though confessing my sins to the priest in church and carried on speaking as the sixth version of myself.

The morning sun shone through the gap in the curtains, extending a straight ray of light over the floor in the dim room. It cut between Masashi and me.

"This dirty, ugly, pathetic, stupid, crazy me is the real me, you know. I'm sure you're disappointed. I'm sorry I've deceived you all this time."

"Do you still hate me so much even now?" He looked bewildered, but his voice was strangely calm.

"I do. Scary, isn't it? Horrible. I know I'm awful, but it's also true that I do love you, Masashi. Creepy, right?"

Masashi flew at me, and for a moment I thought he was attacking me, but no. He hugged me to him.

"This is the real Haruka, isn't it? I'm so happy you decided to show it all, only to me. Thank you!"

I was surprised to see that he was crying. As he covered me in his hug while I knelt there, the ray of light coming from the window shone on him. It looked like a crack splitting him in two.

As he responded to the sixth version of me, a new Masashi was emerging. I was witnessing the precise moment it was happening.

He was operating his muscles in a way he had never done before: the sides of his mouth pulled out, the corners of his lips rising, his nose straightened, the outer corners of his eyes drooped, and his brow furrowed. Having created this face I'd never seen before, he smiled at me.

"I'm sorry you've had to suffer all by yourself until now, Ha-chan. From now on, you can show everything to me, and I'll always provide you with unconditional love. I promise I'll save you!"

"Ha-chan?" I asked blankly.

Masashi covered his face with even more wrinkles as he tried to impress a compassionate smile on me.

"The Ha is from both Haruka and Hannibal Lecter, and adding the diminutive *chan* makes it cute, right? And instead of Masashi, you can call me Ma, as in Mother. It's perfect, don't you think? From now on, I'll be your Ha-chan's Ma. Everything is going to be okay."

Filled with trepidation, I hugged Ma back. I didn't know what else to do, and that was the only response I could think of.

"Ma!"

"Ha-chan!"

We hugged each other tight. The coercive atmosphere in our closeted space left us no other choice.

"Leave everything about the wedding to me, too. Your true nature is our secret, but little by little you'll be able to talk to everyone as the real Ha-chan, won't you? Promise?"

"I guess . . ."

On the table, the pages of the catalog of the new home the two of us would live in following the wedding flipped over in the breeze from the air conditioner. For the rest of our lives we would be living in a closeted space. From now on, we would be Ha-chan and Ma living in the smallest possible community, a couple.

The easygoing, simple, and cheerful Masashi had already been wiped out of our world. He might still exist somewhere where I'm not, but I would never meet him again.

For some reason, tears streamed down my face as I clung to Ma. I really didn't know whether I was playing up my act of responding or mourning the loss of Masashi.

"Ha-chan!"

Noticing my tears, Ma rubbed my back, his face filled with sadness, but also somehow mixed with joy. His hand was giving shape to my outline as he stroked me.

Repressing a scream, Ha-chan closed her eyes in Ma's arms. The ray of light coming through the curtains was extinguished by a black cloud covering the sky outside.